Garden Girls Cozy Mystery Series Book 8

Hope Callaghan

HopeCallaghan.com
Copyright © 2015
All rights reserved.

This book is a work of fiction. Although places mentioned may be real, the characters, names and incidents and all other details are products of the author's imagination and are fictitious. Any resemblance to actual events or actual persons, living or dead is purely coincidental.

No part of this publication may be copied, reproduced in any format, by any means, electronic or otherwise, without prior consent from the copyright owner and publisher of this book. The only exception is brief quotations in printed reviews.

Visit my website for new releases and special offers: HopeCallaghan.com

Thank you, Peggy Hyndman and Wanda Downs, for taking the time to preview *Bully in the Burbs,* for the extra sets of eyes and for catching all my mistakes.

TABLE OF CONTENTS

Chapter 1

The tick-tock of the wall clock was about to drive Gloria insane. She stared at the minute hand as it slowly inched along, second by agonizingly slow second. She sucked in a deep breath and then slowly let it out. "Whew..."

Liz, Gloria's older sister, slammed her open palm on the kitchen table. "Will you *please* stop doing that? I'm already nervous as a tic!"

Margaret, Gloria's friend, jumped in. "Both of you, we need to exercise a little patience. David should be calling any minute now."

Three sets of eyes turned to stare at the clock again.

Liz pushed her chair back and jumped to her feet. Her eyes narrowed as she studied the dime store rooster clock that hung on the bulkhead above Gloria's sink. "Is that what I think it is?"

Gloria started to giggle, which turned into a belly laugh. The stress of waiting for David to call was causing her to crack under the pressure.

Liz, Margaret and Gloria had unearthed some rare coins at Aunt Ethel's family farm in the Smoky Mountains several months ago. Liz had done some preliminary research on the coins and discovered they were worth money – a lot of money.

The coins had been evenly divided: two for David, Ethel's son, two for Liz, two for Margaret, two for Gloria and last, but not least, two for Sandy McGee, who may or may not have had a legal right to the coins, but to avoid future hassles, they had all unanimously decided to include her in the split.

The State of Tennessee claimed they owned the rare coins and there had been a fierce battle waging in the courts for months now between the five of them and the state.

David had phoned Gloria yesterday and asked her to round up Liz and Margaret for a 10:00 a.m. conference call. The courts had reached a decision.

Gloria had tried to weasel the verdict out of David but he flat out refused, explaining it was best to give them the news at the same time, which is why they were sitting in Gloria's kitchen at 9:58 a.m., waiting with baited breath for his call.

Gloria had hidden her two coins in plain sight and that was what Liz had just noticed. She had stuck the coins inside her kitchen clock. One coin was on 12 and the other on the six.

Gloria plucked the cordless phone from its base and set the phone on the table between the three of them. The group stared at the silent phone, each of them lost in their own thoughts.

Gloria saw this as a blessing and a curse. Her life was almost perfect. She had all that she needed – her family and her friends. She and

Paul, the man of her dreams, had just gotten engaged. To her, this windfall might very well be the worst thing that could ever happen. Money changed people, changed attitudes. What would happen when word got out that they had all this money?

No, it would surely upset the applecart. She was certain the others at the table had the exact same thoughts.

She glanced at Margaret out of the corner of her eye. Margaret would probably fare best. Her husband was a retired banker, although the fact that she'd known there was the possibility of inheriting a windfall and had not mentioned it to Don, her husband, could pose problems for her friend.

Next, she glanced at Liz. At least Liz didn't have to explain herself to anyone, but Liz was single. Gloria could just envision both married and unmarried men coming out of the woodwork to court her. How could she ever find true love?

4

If she were Liz, she would always wonder if the man loved her for who she was or loved her for her money.

This was turning into a real pickle!

Liz slammed her fist on the tabletop in frustration, which caused Gloria to jump. "You're going to give me a heart attack!"

Briing! All three women reached for the phone that sat in the middle of the table. Gloria got to it first. "Hello?"

"Yes! Hi David! You don't say!" Gloria was messing with the other two. David had just asked her to put him on speaker.

Liz yanked the phone from Gloria's hand and gave her hard look. She jammed her thumb on the speaker button and set the phone in the middle of the table.

"Go ahead, David. We're all listening now!" Liz glared at her sister.

Gloria stuck her tongue out at Liz who promptly gave her the bird.

"Stop bickering this instant," Margaret hissed. "We're ready," she told David.

"Great!" His deep voice boomed through the fuzzy line. "I have some good news and some bad news."

"Start with the good news." Margaret wanted to savor at least a moment of happiness.

"The court ruled in our favor. The coins are ours to keep!"

Liz shrieked.

Margaret clutched at her chest.

Gloria twisted her brand spanking new princess-cut diamond engagement ring around her finger. The first person who came to mind was Paul, her fiancé. Her second thought was of her children.

The girl's joyous moment was short-lived. "So what's the bad news?" Liz asked.

"Inheritance tax. The government is going to get their share, one way or another," he said.

"How much is the inheritance tax?" Liz wondered aloud.

"Forty percent," David and Margaret answered in unison. Margaret had already done preliminary research.

Gloria was shocked. "You mean if the coins are worth, say $2 million, the government gets $800k of that right off the top?"

The girls could hear David's laborious sigh over the phone line. "Yep. The good news is you don't live in Japan where the inheritance tax is a whopping 55%."

That did little to make the girls feel better. Still, they would each end up with a cool million, minimum.

Gloria's head was spinning. She missed part of what David said. "...the auction house in New York."

Gloria tried to focus. "I'm sorry, David, I missed what you just said."

"That's okay, Gloria. I'm sure this is a lot to absorb at once. I said that Heritage Auctions in New York is your best bet to get the most bang for your buck if you sell the coins."

All eyes turned to Liz, who had been in charge of locating auction companies. "I've got it covered," she winked, "I've already set up an account."

The conversation ended with the girls thanking David for all of the hard work he'd put into winning the case.

"We need to do something extra nice for him," Margaret said, after the line disconnected.

The room grew silent, each of the girls in deep thought.

Liz spoke first. "I say we wait 24-hours before we breathe a word, so that we can give it time to sink in." She slid out of the kitchen chair and headed for the door with Margaret and Gloria trailing behind.

"Good idea," Gloria agreed.

Gloria and Mally stood on the porch and watched as Margaret and Liz climbed into their vehicles and pulled out onto the main road.

Deep down, Gloria had always thought this day would never come, that somehow the government would find a way to claim ownership of the coins.

Liz had told them before she left that the last quote the auction house had given her was a flat 12% commission for selling the coins. The representative also said that the coins could go for as low as $1.8 million and as high as a cool $2.5 million for two coins.

Gloria wandered over to her desk in the corner of the dining room and pulled out the chair. Sound asleep on top of the chair was Gloria's cat, Puddles. She lifted her cat and settled him on her lap. He opened one eye for a quick glance before he closed it again and fell back asleep.

Gloria did some quick calculations on her desktop calculator and at $1.8 million after the auction house's commission and the government's inheritance tax, she would end up with less than a million bucks!

Almost half the money would go to pay taxes and commissions. Gloria still had a hard time swallowing the amount of taxes she would have to pay.

She spent the rest of the afternoon mulling over how to divide the windfall. After contemplating several different scenarios, she decided to split half amongst her three children, with a stipulation that a percentage of the money go into college funds for all four of her grandchildren.

The other half would be for Paul and her to keep since they planned to marry later that year. Now it was time for her to break the news!

Chapter 2

Gloria paced the kitchen floor of her old farmhouse nervously. She glanced at the clock every few minutes. The girls had sold the coins a few days earlier and after taxes and commissions paid to the auction house; she had netted a cool $1.1 million. One million, one hundred seventy-five thousand, three hundred sixty dollars and twelve cents to be exact.

She had told her children and Paul about the coins and the money, and then explained to each of them her plan to divide the windfall. She was proud that there was nary a gripe or groan from any of them. They all took it quite calmly, even calmer than Gloria herself had hoped.

If Gloria's announcement had surprised Paul, he had done an excellent job of hiding it. He told her whatever she felt was best was what she should do. They had almost $600k to invest, to take care of much-needed repairs around the farms – both his farm and hers - and to take a nice long honeymoon...

That left $196k for each of her children. Gloria had wired Ben's money to an account that he and his wife, Kelly, shared. She also wired money to her son, Eddie, and his wife, Karen's, account.

That left her daughter, Jill, and her husband, Greg. They were on their way over.

Gloria stopped wearing a hole in her kitchen linoleum and Mally and she wandered out to the back porch to wait.

Fall had come early and there was a brisk chill in the air. She gazed at the thick carpet of leaves that covered the ground. Perhaps she could have her grandsons, Tyler and Ryan, over for the weekend to help rake the leaves...

The sound of gravel crunching on the drive caught her attention and she watched the familiar dark sedan pull into the drive. Four doors popped open. Her grandsons raced across the yard to reach their beloved Grams first, while Greg and Jill brought up the rear.

The boys hugged Gloria, and then ran off to check on the tree fort they had built during their last overnight visit. Tyler and Ryan scampered up the ladder and disappeared inside.

Gloria opened the porch door and waited while her daughter and son-in-law stepped into the kitchen.

The check was on the kitchen table, under the glass sugar bowl sitting in the center. Gloria plucked the check from under the bowl and handed it to Jill.

Gloria hadn't told Jill the exact amount and she had asked her sons to keep it quiet. She wanted it to be a surprise and it was, judging by the look on Jill's face.

Her daughter swallowed hard and handed the check to Greg. The color drained from his face and his hand started to shake. He looked up at Gloria. "Are you sure? I mean, this is a lot of money..."

Gloria nodded. "Yes. One hundred percent sure. This is for you to use as you see fit. The only thing I ask is that you set aside some of the money for each of the boys' college funds."

It finally began to sink in. Jill's eye lit. "Greg! We can move! We can finally move into a bigger house!"

Gloria smiled. Greg and Jill had outgrown their small two bedroom bungalow years ago, but money had been tight and with the downturn in the economy, Greg's company had all but eliminated overtime hours, which meant no extra income. The couple was able to make ends meet but there wasn't much left over at the end of the month and certainly not enough money to buy a larger, more expensive home.

"I think that's a wonderful idea," Gloria agreed.

The boys stampeded up the steps and burst through the kitchen door. "We're hungry."

Gloria reached for Tyler and hugged him tight. "I'm hungry, too," she declared. "Let's head down to Dot's. My treat."

"Dot's" was Dot's Restaurant, the only restaurant in the small town of Belhaven. Dot Jenkins, Gloria's close friend, and her husband, Ray, had owned the restaurant for decades.

The five of them climbed into Greg and Jill's car. Gloria squeezed in the backseat, smack dab in the middle of her grandsons. The drive to town was short and she didn't mind being squished between two of her favorite people.

It was just shy of 5 o'clock and the dinner onslaught had not yet begun. The five of them wandered in the front entrance and made their way to the back.

Dot spied the group and after a quick stop in the kitchen, made a beeline for the booth, water glasses in hand. She also had two chocolate milkshakes – one for Tyler and one for Ryan.

"Thank you, Mrs. Jenkins," Tyler said.

"Yeah, thanks!" Ryan reached for his milkshake, grabbed the straw and then took a big sip. "We're rich," he informed Dot.

Dot chuckled. She tucked the empty tray under her arm. "You're rich? Can I borrow some money?" she teased.

Ryan nodded. "Yep. You can borrow some from Grams, too."

Dot winked at Gloria. She knew all about the money. The whole town of Belhaven was talking about the girls' newfound wealth. Heck, all of Montbay County was abuzz!

Dot was happy for her friends. If anyone deserved to have fortune smile down on them, it was Gloria!

"We're gonna buy a new house," Tyler said.

Gloria raised a brow. She didn't think the boys had listened to their conversation. She remembered a saying her mom liked to quote, *"Little pitchers have big ears."*

"That sounds wonderful," Dot said.

"I'm starving," Tyler stuck the bottom of the menu in his mouth and chewed the corner.

"Stop that!" Jill grabbed the menu and yanked it out of his hands.

Dot covered her mouth to hide her grin. "Our special today is all-you-can-eat-tacos."

"Sounds perfect." Gloria hadn't bothered looking at the menu. She knew the entire menu by heart.

"I'll have tacos, too," Ryan piped up. "I can eat at least seventeen," he predicted.

Gloria tapped the tabletop with her fingernails. "Are you sure that's all? You said you were starving."

Ryan ran his hand over his cropped locks. "Yeah...make that twenty."

"Got it," Dot nodded solemnly and winked at Gloria. "Tacos for everyone?"

Gloria wondered if Dot was using Alice's spicy recipe that she had shared with her not long ago.

Alice was her friend, Andrea's, former housekeeper and new roommate. She made some mean Mexican dishes that Gloria adored but that didn't adore Gloria quite as much.

She decided to splurge and try them anyway. After all, they were tacos. How deadly could lettuce, tomato, cheese and a little meat be?

Dot jotted down their order and headed to the back. Gloria turned to Jill. "Will you stay in Green Springs?" Jill had mentioned several times that they would like to move to the larger town of nearby Rapid Creek.

Greg and Jill exchanged a glance

"I'm sure you need to talk it over," Gloria said.

"I don't wanna move," Ryan whined as he kicked the bottom of the booth.

Tyler lifted his shake and took a big gulp that left a chocolate moustache on his upper lip. He wiped it away with the back of his hand. "Me either. I want to live in our house forever!"

"We'll discuss this later." Jill gave the boys one of those "don't-mess-with-mom" looks and the boys grew silent.

Gloria frowned. She had hoped the money would be a blessing, not divide their family!

Thankfully, the food arrived and they got off the subject of a new house and onto Paul and Gloria's upcoming wedding. She had already decided that her youngest grandson, Ryan, would be ring bearer while her two older grandsons, Tyler and Oliver, would be ushers.

Ariel, Gloria's only granddaughter, would be the flower girl.

Although she didn't plan to have a large wedding – just family and friends – she wanted her grandchildren to be part of it and feel important.

Jill spooned hot sauce on her taco and lifted it to her mouth. "Have you decided on a location?"

Gloria frowned. She hadn't gotten that far in the planning stage. She could have Pastor Nate marry them at her church, the Church of God in Belhaven. They had planned a winter wedding, over the holidays, when all of Gloria's children would be in town.

She had two months to work out the details and in the meantime, make room for Paul to move in. They had decided to divide their time between Paul's farm a few miles away and Gloria's farm, just outside the small town of Belhaven.

With the money from the sale of the coins, she had decided to take care of some much-needed repairs on her old place, including a fresh coat of paint and new flooring. The farmhouse's electrical and wiring had never been updated. James, Gloria's first husband, had said years ago that he was concerned that the old wiring was a fire hazard.

Paul's family farm was in similar condition and she had offered to do some updates on his place, as well.

Other than that and a nice honeymoon, she wasn't sure how to spend the rest of the money. Maybe she could set it aside for a rainy day or an emergency.

"I'm not sure where the wedding will take place," Gloria confessed, "I guess we should decide soon."

Jill waved a hand. "Oh, you've got plenty of time, Mom. You have a whole ten weeks or so," she teased.

Beads of sweat formed on Gloria's brow. Ten weeks? That was it?

Jill recognized the look on her mother's face. She reached over and squeezed her hand. "Don't worry, Mom. I'll help out."

Dot was back and had overhead the tail end of the conversation. "We'll all help, Gloria. Don't stress yourself out over this."

They were right. Gloria's close-knit group of friends would give her a hand.

Dot lifted the dirty plates and piled them on her tray. "Why don't you have it at Andrea's place?"

Gloria's eyes widened. Why hadn't she thought of that? Andrea had a lovely tearoom inside her newly remodeled home. It would be perfect for a winter wedding!

After dinner, the five of them wandered to the car and Greg drove back to the farm. During the short drive home, the boys begged Gloria to let them spend the night but Jill was firm.

Tomorrow was a school day and they needed to be in their own beds.

"How about a week from Saturday night? I need someone to help rake all those leaves in the yard. I'll even pay you."

Tyler shot as far forward in his seat as his seatbelt would allow and grabbed his mom's shoulder. "Can we, Mom? Can we stay at Grams?"

Jill glanced at her mother. "If she wants you to."

The matter was settled. The boys would spend the night and help rake the yard, burn leaves and still have plenty of time to play in the tree fort. It would work out perfectly since it might be the last chance Gloria had time to spend with them before the holidays and life got too hectic.

Gloria hugged each of her grandsons before she climbed out of the car. She watched the car disappear from sight before she headed to the back porch.

It was still early evening but already dark. The days were growing shorter and although she welcomed the changing season and looked forward to the months ahead, she wished the daylight hours lasted a little longer.

Gloria prayed for her children as she locked the porch door behind her. She prayed that God would find them the perfect house.

Change was hard, particularly for young boys who would have to move away from friends and everything familiar.

Chapter 3

The days flew by as Gloria arranged for electricians to inspect both Paul's farm and her farm. She brought in several local companies to give her quotes to replace the worn linoleum in the kitchen and bath and to put down new wood floors in the dining room.

Greg and Jill had previewed several homes in Rapid Creek and her daughter had called her mother the day before yesterday to let Gloria know that the offer on the home they had fallen in love with had been accepted.

Jill was excited to have her mom look at the home and Gloria couldn't wait to see it. Even the boys started to get excited after they saw the place. They would each have their own room instead of sharing a room.

Gloria pulled Annabelle into Jill's drive and parked off to the side. It was the middle of the week and the boys were in school. The plan was for Gloria and her daughter to look at the house then have lunch together to discuss the upcoming move.

The closing date on the house was exactly one week before Thanksgiving. A lot needed to happen in a short amount of time and Gloria had offered to do whatever it took to help her family.

A harried Jill met Gloria at the door.

Gloria peeked over her shoulder. The house was in shambles. Boxes filled every inch of available space, leaving only a small path from the door, through the kitchen and beyond.

"You don't want to go in there," Jill warned.

Gloria believed her. She herself hadn't moved in years but she had helped plenty of friends and moving was one of Gloria's least favorite things to do. That and paint.

Her plan was to live on the farm until she breathed her last. The kids would have to worry about the rest.

Jill grabbed her car keys and she followed her mother to the car. Green Springs, where Jill currently lived, was a short ten-minute drive to the new house in Rapid Creek.

The town of Rapid Creek was both charming and historical. Many of the town's original structures remained. A small, touristy area lined the side of the creek and at the end of the shops was an old flourmill a local had turned into a popular restaurant and bakery, The Old Mill.

In the summer, a small livery rented canoes, kayaks and inner tubes to area residents who were brave enough to plunge into the icy waters of the clear, cool creek.

When Gloria was young, such a place didn't exist. Instead, they made do with old tire tubes that they would drag to the edge of the water and then hop in from the banks of the river.

They drove past Main Street, crossed over the river and headed up the hill to the other side of town where several small neighborhoods had sprouted up in recent years.

Jill steered the car to the right and into one of the neighborhoods, "Highland Park."

"I still can't believe the deal we got on this place," Jill chattered excitedly, "four bedrooms, two full baths and even a half bath, plus a two car garage. The lot is almost a quarter acre and the house is less than ten years old."

Jill turned down a side street, "Pine Place."

"It even has a stone fireplace in the living room!"

They pulled into a drive near the end of the cul-de-sac. "Here it is!"

The front of the house was brick.

The first thing Gloria noticed was the large picture window in front, covered by an expansive porch, perfect for a pair of rocking chairs.

Jill reached for the door handle. "I can't wait to show you the inside!"

Gloria was that they were spending the money wisely. "How much did you say this house cost?"

"Only $125,000. Can you believe it? Houses in this neighborhood are selling for closer to $200,000."

Gloria had prayed about finding the right place. It appeared as if God had answered her prayers.

The real estate agent had given Jill the code to unlock the lockbox that hung on the front door knob. She punched in the code, pulled out the key and unlocked the front door.

A small foyer opened up into a large living room with vaulted ceilings. Tall, cherry-stained bookshelves flanked a large, stone fireplace.

Light oak covered the floors and continued into the kitchen and dining room, all open and within view of the living room. It was a popular, modern floor plan and a good fit for Jill and the boys. Her daughter could keep a close eye on them from the main living area.

On the other side of the kitchen was a small hall that led out to the garage. A laundry room was off to the left of the kitchen and a small half bath to the right.

Jill pointed to the bath. "This will be perfect to keep the boys from running through the house with dirty shoes."

Gloria nodded to the laundry room. "You can strip 'em down at the door."

They wandered back into the kitchen. Gloria ran her hand lightly across the dark granite counters. They were beautiful. The kitchen was an ample size and sported a large center island with enough room for several barstools.

The kitchen appliances were all stainless steel and looked almost new.

Gloria spun around. "I love this kitchen." She touched the counters again, "especially these countertops."

"You should put them in your kitchen," Jill told her.

It was a thought. The granite was beautiful. The counters she had now worked just fine but James had put them in back in the 70's and they were apricot orange. Through the years and the kids, they had accumulated several chips and scuffs, and many memories along the way... "Perhaps I don't need new ones after all," she decided.

They started to pass by the kitchen on their way to the bedrooms in the back when something on the back counter caught Gloria's eye. It was a sheet of paper, folded in half. "What's that?"

Jill shook her head. "I don't know. What is it?"

Jill stepped to the counter and picked up the paper. She opened it up. Gloria peeked over her shoulder.

"Beware! This house is cursed. Death awaits."

Jill released her grip on the note and it fluttered to the floor. "What in the world?"

Gloria slipped her reading glasses on, bent down and picked up the note. "Someone is trying to scare you."

"Someone that has been in this house." Jill glanced around nervously.

Gloria didn't reply. She walked over to the service door that connected the garage to the kitchen and twisted the knob. The door was locked.

Next, she stepped into the laundry room and pushed up on the window sash. Locked.

She moved from room-to-room, checking each window and door. The entire upper floor was secure, the girls descended the center staircase to the lower level, and stepped into the walkout basement.

Gloria flicked the lights on and gazed around the room. It was an enormous, open area, perfect for her grandsons to play and roughhouse without breaking anything.

Gloria's ears burned at the thought that someone was trying to scare her family from buying the house! She marched across the room and down a long hall. At the end of the hall was a large bedroom. She stomped over to the window, grabbed the sash and yanked. The window easily lifted. Cool, fall air rushed in.

Jill shuffled in behind her.

Gloria turned. "See? Someone snuck in and left that note, hoping to frighten you."

Jill shivered and rubbed her upper arms. "They did a good job."

Gloria pulled the window closed and clicked the lock in place. They checked the rest of the windows then headed back up the stairs.

Jill led her mom through the garage and service door into the back yard. Two large, oak trees sat near the back. Off to one side were the remnants of a garden. A tiered wooden deck that looked brand new covered the back of the house.

They wandered back through the garage and into the kitchen. "Do not let this scare you, Jill."

Jill frowned at the note, still on the counter. "I'm going to call the real estate agent as soon as I get home. Maybe she knows something about this house or neighborhood."

She folded the note and shoved it into her purse. "I knew it was too good to be true!"

The girls stopped at The Old Mill to grab a bite to eat. Jill picked at her food. Gloria knew the note bothered her daughter. She tried to reason with her but once Jill got something in her head that was it. She would agree or go along with what you said, but all the time her plan was to do the complete opposite.

The entire trip back to Jill's place, Gloria tried to convince her daughter it was nothing.

Gloria followed Jill into the house. "Call the agent so you can clear this up and quit worrying."

Jill dialed the number and put the phone on speaker. Luckily, the agent was in the office and it was a short time before her agent, Sue Camp, picked up the line. "Hello Jill," a cheery voice greeted them.

"Hi Sue. I have you on speaker. My mom and I just came back from the house."

"Oh good! I'm sure your mother approves of the lovely home."

"She does," Jill agreed, "but now I'm not sure anymore."

The cheer turned to alarm. "You're kidding. Why not?"

Jill explained how they found the note on the counter. She told the real estate agent what the note said and that they discovered an unlocked window on the lower level.

Gloria jumped in. "Gloria, here. This house has been on the market for a long time. At that price and as nice as it is, someone should have snatched it up long ago. Is there something we should know?"

There was a long pause on the other end, so long that Gloria thought the line had disconnected.

"Hello? Are you still there?"

"Yes, I'm still here. There has been an issue with this particular home," Sue Camp admitted.

Chapter 4

Jill tugged on a loose strand of hair. "Wh-what kind of issue?"

"Several other buyers have gone to contract on this house, only to back out days later."

"Because?" Gloria asked. Getting this woman to talk was like pulling teeth!

"Oh, threatening notes and other small nitpicky things."

"Such as?" Gloria prompted – again!

"Desumbap." Unintelligible reply.

"What did you say?"

There was a heavy sigh on the other end. "I said some dead, rotting animals keep popping up on the porch."

There was more - Gloria just knew it. "Anywhere else?"

"The deck out back and in the garage."

Gloria had never met Sue Camp, but the woman was starting to get on Gloria's last nerve. "Surely a couple dead animals and threatening notes have not scared buyers to the point that they cancelled." Gloria had another thought. "How many buyers have walked?"

"Seven."

Jill had started to recover from her shock. "Seven buyers in seven months, including us?"

"No. In addition to you."

"I-I'm not sure I want to buy this house," Jill told the woman.

"You'll lose your deposit," the real estate agent warned her.

"She'll call you back." Gloria grabbed the phone and disconnected the line.

Gloria turned to her daughter. "How much was the deposit?"

Jill swallowed hard. "Almost seven thousand dollars."

"Seven thousand dollars – for a deposit?" Gloria had never purchased real estate. Her farm had passed down through the family for generations.

She had friends who had purchased real estate, though, and she knew that an earnest money deposit was small – maybe a thousand or two.

"They wanted to make sure we were serious," Jill whispered in a small voice.

Gloria grabbed her daughter's hand. "C'mon. We're going back to that house for a closer look."

They drove back to the house in silence. Jill was mulling over how she could get out of the contract. Her mother, on the other side of the car, was trying to figure out how to get to the bottom of this!

Jill pulled into the drive and the women climbed out of the car. Jill hung her head and shuffled up the sidewalk.

It broke Gloria's heart to see her daughter so despondent. She had been so excited about the place and now the thrill was gone, replaced by dread, which caused Gloria to be even more determined. Someone was trying to scare them off and she was not going to have any of it!

Gloria stepped inside the front door and right into detective mode. She grabbed her reading glasses from her purse and slipped them on. She studied the walls, the windows and she even pulled the grate from the fireplace and peered inside.

The women made their way into the garage. Gloria opened the cabinets, got down on her hands and knees and looked under the shelves. Her gaze wandered up to the ceiling and to the yellow string attached to the attic ladder.

Gloria grasped the string and pulled. She unfolded the steps and started up. It was dark except for a small amount of light that filtered in through the round louver centered above the garage door.

Nothing appeared to be out of place. Gloria backed down the stairs, folded the steps and pushed the ladder back in place. She dusted her hands and rubbed them on the front of her jeans.

Jill watched in silence, unable to muster enough enthusiasm to help her mother search for clues.

The laundry room was clean. The half bath was clean. Gloria pulled open the cupboard door nearest to the stove. She inspected every drawer and every cupboard in search of something, anything.

Finally, Jill joined her mother and started on the other end of the kitchen. It was a lovely kitchen, bright and beautiful with a large bay window above the stainless steel sink that overlooked the garden and backyard.

Gloria turned her attention to the open dining room on the other side of the kitchen island. A bright beam of sunlight reflected off the freshly painted wall on the far side.

Gloria noticed a faint outline on the wall. "Do you see that?"

"See what?" Jill asked.

Gloria walked over to the wall. She followed the outline with her hand. She took a step back and then stepped to the side. The outline was much clearer from that angle. It was an inverted pentagram.

Gloria had a sneaking suspicion the real estate agent knew all about the pentagram and had kept mum, probably hoping she could finally unload the house and collect her commission!

Gloria felt the steam roll out of her ears. She held out her hand. "Give me your phone. I'm calling Sue Camp."

Jill did as her mother requested. She recognized that look and the tone of her mother's voice and she almost felt sorry for her real estate agent. Almost.

"I'd like to speak with Sue Camp, please," Gloria told the receptionist in a firm voice...a voice that said, "don't even try to tell me she's unavailable."

Sue's calm voice answered. "Hello?"

"Gloria Rutherford, here. I'm Jill Adams' mother. We're back at the house. Were you aware someone has drawn a pentagram on the dining room wall?"

Jill couldn't hear Sue's answer but she cringed anyway.

Gloria responded "Yes" three times in a clipped tone. "Jill will call you back."

No, "Have a nice day." No, "Thank you for your time."

She handed the phone back to her daughter. "That woman knows more than she lets on."

Mother and daughter wandered out the front door. Jill locked the door behind them. "Good-bye house."

"Jill Rutherford Adams, you are not a quitter!"

"I don't want to live in a haunted house!" Jill knew she sounded whiney but she couldn't help it. She wouldn't sleep one wink in that house if she thought for even a second that it was haunted.

Gloria grabbed her daughter's arm. "Let's go meet the neighbors!"

She dragged her reluctant daughter across the lawn to the house next door.

Gloria sucked in a breath and pressed the doorbell. She could hear the faint chime within.

No one answered. She tried a second time then gave up.

They tried the house on the other side. No one answered there either.

"We'll be back," Gloria vowed as they made their way to the car. Neighbors always knew each other's business. If anyone knew the history of the house, it would be the people next door.

Gloria climbed in the passenger seat and fastened her seatbelt. Jill closed the driver's side door and slid the key in the ignition. She looked as if she was about to burst into tears. All she could think about was that her dream home was slipping away and she had just wasted over seven thousand dollars – on nothing!

"Give me seven days," Gloria bargained. "Do not cancel your contract for seven days."

Jill didn't have a choice but to agree to give it a week. After all, she wouldn't have even had a shot at a new home if not for her mother's generosity. "Okay," she relented.

Gloria reached over and patted her hand. "In the meantime, find a new real estate agent and start looking at other homes. That way, if this one doesn't work out, which I am almost 100% certain it will because I'll get to the bottom of this," Gloria vowed, "you'll have a head start."

"Okay?"

Jill had nothing to lose. She quickly agreed. "You have yourself a deal," she said. They drove back to Jill's house in silence. Jill eased into the drive and put the car in park. "Just promise me one thing."

"What's that?" Gloria asked.

"That you won't do anything foolish...like stake out a haunted house in the middle of the night by yourself."

"I won't," Gloria promised. No way would she be brave enough to tackle that alone. Now if she had someone with her? Maybe.

Chapter 5

Gloria left Jill's place and headed home. Downtown Belhaven was packed. Gloria swerved into the post office parking lot and squeezed into the last open spot. She scooted out of the car and made a beeline for the front door.

Gloria's friend and Head Postmaster, Ruth Carpenter, was behind the counter helping a customer.

Gloria wandered over to the wall covered with flyers, showing pictures of missing persons. She was glad that Milton Tilton's mug was not one of the pictures.

Gloria and her friends had recently helped solve the case and had rescued poor Milt, which reminded her that she needed to call her sister, Liz.

Liz was a spendthrift and Gloria thought that maybe she could give her sister a few pointers on investing her money.

Ruth finished the transaction and the customer headed toward the exit. It was Patti Palmer. Patti scowled at Gloria, stuck her nose in the air and walked right past her without uttering a word.

Gloria watched as she exited the post office and slammed the door behind her.

"Yeah. I think she's still a little miffed," Ruth observed.

Gloria sniffed and shrugged her shoulders. "It's not my fault her son is a criminal!"

She changed the subject. "Jill is in a pickle." She went on to explain the dilemma. "Something is rotten in Denmark and I plan to get to the bottom of it," Gloria vowed.

Ruth, always willing to offer a helping hand since Gloria had gotten her out of some tight spots, not the least of which was drug trafficking charges. "I'd love to help but haunted houses freak me out."

"Supposedly haunted," Gloria corrected. "I have my doubts."

Ruth tapped her fingernails on the counter top. "Let me know if I can help in some other way." She shivered. "The place is already giving me the creeps and I haven't even been there."

"Thanks for the offer." Gloria headed for the door. "Say, what do you think about Paul and me getting married over at Andrea's place?"

"In her new tearoom?" Ruth smiled. "That would be the perfect spot!"

Gloria nodded. "That's what I thought." She stepped out of the post office and quietly closed the door.

She hopped into Annabelle and fired up the engine.

Gloria headed out of town. She started to pass by her best friend, Lucy's, place and made a last minute decision to stop in.

Lucy's bright yellow jeep was in the drive. Behind her jeep was another car – one that looked vaguely familiar but that Gloria couldn't quite place.

Gloria pulled the car behind the jeep and shut the engine off.

She climbed out of the car and stepped onto the sidewalk.

Whaam!

Gloria recognized the sound. It was the sound of explosives. Lucy was at it again!

She stepped off the sidewalk and made her way toward the shed in the back of the yard.

"No! You gotta stand like this, with your feet apart, so you can keep your balance. Otherwise, the gun is gonna kick back and knock you on your rear."

Lucy, in full camo gear, wearing eye goggles and earplugs, demonstrated her stance to the man standing next to her – Lucy's new boyfriend, Max Field.

Max nodded. He followed Lucy's example and did as she told him. Max lifted the gun.

Gloria covered her ears.

Boom!

Max lowered the gun. Lucy patted him on the back. "Much better," she told him.

Gloria started to clap. "Bravo! Bravo!"

Lucy and Max whirled around. The gun in Max's hand pointed right at Gloria.

Gloria's threw both hands in the air. "Don't shoot!"

Max cringed. He lowered the gun. "Sorry Gloria."

With the gun safely at Max's side, Gloria stepped closer. "Is Lucy teaching you how to blow stuff up?"

Lucy was an adrenaline junkie. If she wasn't jumping out of planes, she was racing across her back field on her four wheeler. She had recently taken a hankering to building small explosives and then using them for target practice.

She tried several times to get Gloria to join in the "fun" but Gloria drew the line at blowing stuff up.

Gloria kept a small handgun in her dresser drawer. Thanks to Lucy, Gloria had become a good shot. If an intruder broke into her house and threatened her, she was confident she would be able to protect herself.

Max set the gun on top of the tree trunk next to him before he removed the safety goggles and earplugs. "Yeah. I guess I am getting better. This time I didn't shoot out her window."

He nodded to a small window frame at the corner of the shed...one without glass. "Thank goodness I found someone who is able to come by here on Monday to fix it."

Lucy picked up the earplugs and goggles and set them on the workbench inside the shed before she returned. "You didn't have to do that, Max. I could have just as easily boarded it up. That way, if you accidentally hit it again, it won't matter."

He nodded. She had a point...although he was getting better with his aim. Max glanced at his watch. "I better take off. I'm meeting the guys for a round of golf over in Green Springs."

Lucy walked Max to his car while Gloria waited by the shed. She watched as they disappeared around the old oak tree and out of sight.

Gloria liked Max. He seemed a much better fit than Bill, Lucy's ex-boyfriend. Lucy met Max during their last case, when Milton Tilton had come up missing. Max and Milt were friends.

Max's sport car pulled out onto the road and Lucy met her friend in the rear yard. Gloria waited while Lucy put the gun and explosives in the shed.

Gloria followed her inside and watched as Lucy stood in front of a small sink and washed her hands.

"You put a sink in the shed?"

Lucy squeezed a glob of dish soap on her hands and rubbed them together. "Yeah. I decided it was best if I got the gunpowder residue off my hands before going in the house. Don't want to blow up the inside of my house."

She dried her hands on a towel nearby then closed the door to the shed. "What brings you to my neck of the woods?"

Gloria explained the situation with Jill's house as they wandered up the back porch steps and into the kitchen. "Something fishy is going on over there at Highland Park. Someone is trying to scare Jill away from that house and they're doing a darn good job."

Lucy reached for a box of peanut brittle sitting on top of the fridge. She lifted the lid and held it out. "Want some?"

Gloria shook her head. "No thanks, although it looks delicious."

Lucy grabbed a piece and closed the lid. "Did you say Highland Park?"

"Yeah. The house is in Rapid Creek. In a neighborhood called Highland Park."

Lucy crunched on a chunk of the hard candy. "I think RJ and his wife, Carol, live there."

"Really?"

RJ was Randall, Jr., Dot and Ray Jenkins', nephew. RJ was almost like a son to them. He was about the same age as Gloria's children and growing up, the kids had all been close.

"I'll give her a call later to see if I can get RJ's number. Maybe he knows of odd occurrences that have happened in the neighborhood or that house."

Gloria eyed the box of peanut brittle.

Lucy grinned and slid the box toward her. "Changed your mind, huh?"

Gloria lifted the lid and took a small piece. She bit the end. It was delicious and almost melted in Gloria's mouth. "Did I tell you Liz is moving to Florida?"

"Nope." If the news surprised Lucy, it didn't show. Of course, everyone knew Liz was impulsive so it probably wasn't a surprise. "She's taking all that money and hitting the road."

Gloria eyed the box of peanut brittle, her small piece long gone. She swept a hand across her extra tummy roll. If she was going to lose a few pounds before the wedding, she needed to stop eating all the goodies.

What Gloria said next, did surprise Lucy. "Frances is going with her."

Lucy lifted a brow. "Is she taking Milt?" Lucy had been part of Milt's search and rescue mission. She knew all about Frances' extreme obsession with the man.

"Nope. Milt ran off to Vegas and got married."

Lucy's jaw dropped. "No way!"

"Yes way. I haven't seen Frances," Gloria shook her head, "but I can just imagine she's fit to be tied."

"You'll never guess who he married." Gloria was about to tell Lucy but her phone chirped. Gloria opened her purse and stuck her hand in. She turned the front so that it faced her and squinted at the screen. It was Jill.

"Hello?"

There was no one there. Gloria had just missed the call.

She started to dial her back when she noticed that Jill had left a message.

Gloria punched in the access code and turned it to speaker. "Hi Mom. I wanted to let you know that Greg and I found another house that we like. I told Sue that I needed to talk to you before I put in an offer."

The rest of the message was brief. Gloria frowned and dropped the phone inside her purse. She didn't want to see Jill lose all that money and the house of her dreams.

"I guess you better get cracking on the case," Lucy said.

Gloria shoved the kitchen chair back and jumped to her feet. "Yeah and the sooner the better. I guess I need to head back into town and talk to Dot."

Lucy followed her to her car. "Let me know if you need help with the investigation," Lucy offered.

Gloria thanked her, climbed into the car and backed out of the driveway.

She pulled Annabelle into an open spot and turned the car off before calling her daughter back. "Tomorrow. Give me until noon tomorrow," she bargained. "Stall the agent, whatever you have to do."

Jill finally relented and Gloria knew she needed to get a move on.

Gloria stepped inside the restaurant and scanned the room. Dot was nowhere around.

Ray, Dot's husband, who had just poured coffee at a nearby table, walked across the dining room. "Dot had a doctor's appointment earlier."

He shifted the coffee carafe to his other hand. "You can check the house. She's probably back by now."

Gloria thanked him and headed back out the door.

Ray and Dot lived a few short blocks from the restaurant, which was a good thing since they spent most of their waking hours working.

Dot's dark blue van was in the drive. Gloria pulled in behind her and wandered up the steps to the front door.

She rang the front bell and waited. The curtain rustled and Dot peeked out before she opened the door.

Gloria took one look at her friend's face and knew something was wrong. "What is it?"

"Uh..." Dot shook her head but the look was still plastered across her face.

Gloria adjusted her purse and crossed her arms in front of her. "Something is wrong, Dot Jenkins. It's written all over your face."

Dot's face turned red. She closed her eyes and swayed back, as if she might go over.

Gloria grabbed her arm to steady her. "Are you okay?"

Dot shook her head. "I don't know."

That was all Gloria needed to hear. She placed a protective arm around her friend's shoulder and led her into the living room.

"Come on. Let's go to the kitchen," she urged.

Gloria led her into the kitchen. She pulled out a chair and Dot settled in. She promptly dropped her face in her hands.

Gloria's heart sunk. She had never seen Dot so discombobulated, unless she counted the time that someone died at the restaurant after eating Dot's dumplings.

Dot was the most levelheaded, analytical, and thoughtful one of their group of friends. Her feathers were rarely ruffled. It was always smooth sailing in Dot's world.

"Coffee. I'll make some coffee." Gloria was as familiar with Dot's kitchen as she was her own. She reached into the cupboard, pulled down a Tupperware container full of freshly ground coffee along with a stack of filters.

Gloria filled the empty glass pot with water. After she dropped a filter in the top, she dumped a scoop of coffee on top. She turned the switch to "on" and whirled around to face her friend.

Dot was in the same position: her head in her hands and her shoulders slumped.

"Dot," Gloria kneeled next to Dot's chair, "talk to me."

Dot lifted her head. Her face was pale, her lips pinched and her expression blank. "The doctor..."

Her voice trailed off.

Gloria remembered Ray telling her that Dot had gone to the doctor earlier.

Call it a sixth sense. Call it a premonition, or call it a knowing your friend so well that somehow Gloria knew what was coming next.

Dot took a deep breath. "I have cancer."

Chapter 6

The words hung heavy in the air. It was as if, for a moment, time stood still. Gloria's mind went blank. She was having trouble wrapping her head around the word cancer.

Finally, she found her voice. "Does..."

Dot slowly shook her head. "No. Ray doesn't know. He didn't even know I had gone in for a biopsy. I didn't want to worry him. I figured it was nothing."

Gloria's mouth flapped open and shut as she tried to digest the news. "Why didn't you..."

"...ask one of you to go with me?" Dot shrugged. "Same reason. I thought it was nothing and I didn't want anyone to worry."

The coffee had finished brewing. Gloria jerked forward like a robot. Her body went through the motions but her mind was a jumble of emotions.

Cancer. Gloria's mother had cancer. It had taken her slowly, sucking the life out of her one day at a time until there was nothing left. Nothing left but death.

Tears stung the back of Gloria's eyes as she tried desperately to blink them away while she fixed them both a cup of coffee.

She needed to be strong for Dot, for Ray and for herself.

She dumped a packet of creamer and packet of sugar in Dot's cup before she picked it up and carried both cups to the table.

She plastered a smile on her face and set the cup in front of Dot. "You're a fighter, Dot. You're gonna kick this thing's butt!"

Dot smiled hollowly as she faced her dear friend. "Yes, I am." Whether she felt it yet, she wasn't certain, but just saying it out loud made her feel better.

Gloria slid into the kitchen chair and cradled her cup as she listened to Dot pour out her story. She told Gloria as much as she could remember and ended with the doctor wanting to meet with both Dot and Ray the next day to go over her treatment.

After she finished, her eyes dropped to the half-empty cup of coffee.

Gloria grabbed Dot's hand. "Let's pray." She didn't wait for an answer as she bowed her head and poured her heart out to the only one who could help.

"Dear Heavenly Father. Our hearts are heavy this afternoon as we learn about Dot's diagnosis. Lord, we know You are the great physician and we pray that You heal Dot completely. Heal her body and let her be a testament to Your Glory. Amen."

Gloria lifted her head and quoted the first scripture that came to mind.

"Therefore confess your sins to each other and pray for each other so that you may be healed. The prayer of a righteous person is powerful and effective." James 5:16 NIV

Dot reached for a Kleenex to wipe her eyes. "Thank you, Gloria."

Gloria picked up her empty coffee cup, along with Dot's cup and carried them to the sink. She washed the cups, dried them with the towel and placed them back inside the cupboard.

"Now, I'm going to head back to the restaurant and send Ray home. He needs to be with you right now and you two need to talk," Gloria said.

"But..."

Gloria shook her finger at her friend. "No ifs, ands or buts. Holly and I can handle the restaurant," she said. Holly was a part-time employee at the restaurant and Gloria had seen her earlier when she had stopped by to track Dot down.

Gloria wasn't 100% certain she was up to the task but somehow, some way, she was going to help her friend. She grabbed her purse and headed for the front door.

Dot trailed behind.

Gloria impulsively spun around and hugged her friend tightly. She squeezed her eyes shut and willed herself not to burst into tears. "I'll talk to you tomorrow."

She hurried out of the house, afraid she might lose it right then and there.

Dot quietly closed the door behind her.

Inside Dot's restaurant, Gloria charged right down the center aisle and made a beeline for the back. Holly and Ray were in the kitchen.

She dropped her purse on the chair near the door and grabbed an apron from the hook.

Ray pulled a basket of fries from the fryer and hung it on the hook to drain. "You're back. Dot wasn't home?"

Gloria nodded. She reached around to tie the strings in the back. "Yes. She needs you to come home. I'm taking over."

Ray shook his head, confused. "Who will..."

Gloria pointed to Holly. "Holly and I can handle this," she said.

Ray started to argue. Gloria lifted her hand. "Please. Ray. Go home."

The tone of Gloria's voice and the expression on her face finally sunk in. Something was wrong. Terribly wrong.

Ray nodded. He quickly removed his apron and without another word, headed out the rear door.

She watched as he backed his compact car out of the dirt parking lot behind the restaurant and

71

eased the car down the alley. Gloria closed her eyes and prayed for them both.

Holly wedged her fist on her hip. "You think we can pull this off?" she asked doubtfully. "Dinner crunch starts in half an hour."

Gloria reached for her purse – and her cell phone. "It's time to call in the troops."

Gloria went right down the line as she called each of the Garden Girls. She started with Ruth, who was across the street working at the post office. "I'll be over in half an hour, as soon as I lock up here," she promised.

Lucy was next. She could tell by the tone in Gloria's voice she needed help. "I'm on my way," she said.

Last, but not least, was Margaret. For a minute, Gloria thought she wasn't home but she finally picked up. She sounded out of breath. "Sorry, I was out filling the bird feeders."

When Gloria told her there was a slight crisis and she needed help covering for Dot and Ray at the restaurant, Margaret cut her off. "Be there in less than five minutes." She hung up before Gloria could even thank her.

Holly listened to Gloria as she called each of her friends. "I wish I had friends like that," she said wistfully.

The front doorbell tinkled. A few customers had trickled in. Holly held up a finger. "Be right back."

Gloria watched her retreating back and for the first time since she had arrived at the restaurant, she actually began to believe they would survive the day.

When all of the girls arrived at the restaurant minutes later, Gloria herded them into the back. "I can't tell you what is going on; only that Dot and Ray need us right now. We have to run the restaurant tonight and maybe even tomorrow."

None of the girls, other than Holly, had experience working in a restaurant, other than pitching in here or there when Dot was in a pinch and only under her direct supervision. "We've gotta fake it until we can make it," Gloria told them.

The dinner rush had begun and the girls spent the rest of the evening racing around the restaurant, putting out fires, one even literally when Margaret accidentally put the frying pan oil too close to a roll of paper towels and it caught fire. Thankfully, she was able to put it out before it spread.

Hours later, after the last customer walked out the door, the last dish washed and put away; they breathed a collective sigh of relief.

The girls had even managed to do some prep for the next morning's breakfast crowd.

Ray had called earlier to check in and ask how they were doing. Gloria calmly told him they had it under control, although that was not quite all of it. They were running around like chickens with their heads cut off.

Gloria was more than a little relieved when Ray told her his brother, Randall, and his family would open the restaurant the next morning. Randall owned a restaurant up north. The restaurant was only open during the summer months and they had just closed for the season. Randall was also RJ's dad.

In another month, Randall and his wife would head to Florida for the winter.

After she hung up the phone, the girls each grabbed a plate of leftover chicken pot pie and settled into a table near the back.

Lucy was the last to take a seat and the first to speak. "How is Dot?"

Gloria had asked Ray if it was okay for her to tell the other girls about Dot and he said he thought it was a great idea and that it would take a little pressure off Dot.

Gloria explained the situation and when she said the word "cancer," the group gasped, each of them having a reaction similar to hers.

When the news sunk in, they all vowed to do whatever they could to help their dear friend, Dot.

Gloria and Lucy were the last to leave. Gloria locked the back door and followed Lucy down the alley and around front, where they had parked their cars.

Lucy fiddled with her keys, twirling the ring around her finger. "When will we know what the doctor has to say?" she asked Gloria.

"Ray said he would let me know tomorrow. As soon as I know, I'll call everyone," she promised.

Lucy impulsively reached over and hugged Gloria. Dot's unexpected news made her – made them all – cherish their friendships now more than ever.

Back at the farm, Gloria wearily climbed out of Annabelle and wandered up the porch steps. Mally, who was ready to go out, greeted Gloria at the door.

She followed Mally back out to the porch and waited while she raced around the yard, tromped through the garden, watered her favorite tree and wandered back to the porch.

Gloria settled into the rocking chair. Soon, she would have to store the chairs in the barn – before the first snowfall.

Small piles of fallen leaves danced in the yard, taunting her. She knew she needed to rake and burn the leaves but once again, she had so much going on. Between Jill's haunted house and Dot's cancer, she would have her hands full.

Her eyes wandered to the front yard. She could see the branches from the tree out front, the one that was home to her grandsons' tree fort, sticking out. Maybe she could have them over for the afternoon to play in the fort and help rake the leaves.

The tree reminded her that she needed to call Jill back. So much had happened.

Jill picked up on the first ring. "We put an offer in on that other house," Jill told her.

"Did you put down a deposit?" Gloria asked.

"No. The real estate agent said we could wait until the sellers accepted the offer. This deposit would only be $1000."

"So you've given up on the other house?"

Jill sighed deeply. "I love that first house and it kills me to think we're going to lose all that money."

"You know RJ and his wife live in Highland Park," Gloria said. "Maybe I can ask them about the house."

"If you think it would help," Jill said doubtfully, "go ahead."

78

It certainly couldn't hurt. On top of that, RJ would more than likely be at Dot's Restaurant in the morning. She could ask him then. "Good. I'll ask tomorrow."

If Jill put down another deposit and decided to go with house #1 after all, at least she would only lose $1000 on the second house. The other way around, losing house #1, would be a lot more costly. Of course, Gloria didn't want to see her lose a single penny!

Gloria hung up the phone, turned off the kitchen light and headed to the bathroom to brush her teeth. Tomorrow was shaping up to be a busy day and she was whupped!

Chapter 7

The next morning, Dot's Restaurant was a beehive of activity. Gloria drove around the block twice before she gave up on finding an open spot and pulled into the post office parking lot.

She dashed across the busy street and glanced in the front window. Her heart sank when she realized she wouldn't see her friend's familiar figure dart back and forth through the window.

Instead, she saw a tall, lanky man doing the darting. It was Randall.

He caught Gloria's eye when she stepped in the front door and gave a small wave. Gloria made a beeline for the back, nodding to a few of the diners she recognized.

Stacy, Randall's wife, was standing in front of the flat top, cooking pancakes. She turned her attention for a brief moment and smiled. "Hello Gloria."

Gloria returned the smile and glanced around the kitchen. Her eyes settled on RJ, bent over the kitchen sink, up to his elbows in sudsy water.

He caught Gloria's eye. "Ah. I heard you were looking for me."

He turned on the cold tap water and rinsed the bubbles from his arms. "I heard that Jill is thinking of moving to Highland Park. It's a great area," he assured her.

"I'm glad to hear that but she may not move there after all." Gloria explained the situation briefly.

"Have you heard anything about Pine Place that would cause Jill concern about buying that house?"

RJ rubbed the faint stubble on his chin. "What is the address?"

Gloria couldn't remember. She was lucky if she could remember what day of the week it was. She slipped on her glasses, lifted her cell phone and scanned her text messages until she got to the one Jill had sent her with the address. "726 Pine Place."

RJ's eyes widened. "Oh yeah. Now that you mention it, there was a big ruckus over there about six months ago."

RJ went on to explain that the owners of the place Jill and Greg had put an offer on had been running a puppy mill. Some of the neighbors had tipped off local authorities who swooped in and shut it down.

"I think their last name was Acosta." RJ continued. "They got mad and promptly put the house up for sale and now I guess it has been on the market for a while."

Gloria's brow furrowed. Did the owners have something to do with the notes and pentagram painting? Wouldn't they just want to unload the house and move on? Not if they kept collecting huge earnest money deposits from potential buyers.

Gloria remembered that Sue Camp had mentioned that the house had gone pending several times already. Each deal had fallen apart. Seven thousand dollars several times over was a tidy profit!

She made a mental note to do a little more research into the previous owners!

Gloria thanked RJ for his time. She needed to get back over to Highland Park to talk to the neighbors, although it may already be too late and Jill and Greg would move forward with this other house.

Gloria wandered out of the restaurant and headed back to the farm.

She spent the rest of the afternoon on "busy work," which was not much of anything. She couldn't concentrate. All she could think about was poor Dot.

Gloria had just settled in at the kitchen table with a plate of leftover tuna noodle casserole and a small tossed salad when the house phone rang. She paused for a moment, deciding whether to pick up. Maybe it was Dot or Ray...

"Hello?"

"Hi Gloria. I hope I'm not bothering you." It was Dot.

Mally's sniffer honed in on the goodies near the edge of the kitchen table. Gloria reached over and slid the plate to the center. She wagged her finger at her pooch, who slunk off and crawled into her doggie bed near the dining room door.

"What happened?"

She could hear Dot suck in a breath. "It's good news and bad news."

Gloria squeezed her eyes shut. She prayed the good news outweighed the bad.

"The good news is the doctors said they caught the cancer early."

Gloria shuffled over to the kitchen window and peered out into the yard. "And the bad?"

"The surgery is scheduled for week after next and I'm terrified," Dot admitted.

"We'll start a prayer chain today," Gloria said. "Pastor Nate can add you to Sunday's prayer list."

Dot's voice grew thick. "I couldn't even sleep last night. All I could think about was dying."

Gloria's heart sunk. It was moments like this that you just had to hand it all over to the Lord. "Pray about it, Dot. Ask the Lord for peace."

Dot went on. "Anyways, Ray refuses to let me go back to work at the restaurant for the next few days. He thinks it would be too hard on me."

Gloria had to agree. News of Dot's cancer would spread through their small town like wildfire, if it hadn't already. "He's right," she simply said.

Gloria could hear muffled sounds on the other end. Dot was on the move.

"I talked to RJ a little while ago. He told me about the house Jill is trying to buy over in Rapid Creek. It sounds like something fishy is going on."

Gloria didn't want to burden Dot with Jill's crisis but she briefly explained what had happened.

"Are you going stand by and let her lose that money?" If it had been Dot's daughter, she would have tried to get to the bottom of it. Dot knew that Gloria would not simply throw in the towel, so to speak.

"Not if I can help it," Gloria declared. "I'm going over there in the morning and pound on some doors." It would be the perfect day. Saturday morning. People would be home from work...

"Can I go with you?" Dot asked. "I mean, I can't go to the restaurant. What else am I gonna do?"

Gloria frowned. Dot had enough on her mind, but then again, maybe what she needed was to take her mind off the upcoming surgery. "Sure, Dot. If that's what you want to do."

She glanced at the wall clock. If they got there around ten, most people should be up and about. "I can swing by around 9:30 tomorrow morning and pick you up."

"Thanks, Gloria. I'd like that."

Gloria's cell phone chirped. Someone was trying to call but Gloria didn't want to cut Dot off so she let it ring. Whoever was trying to call could leave a message.

The girls chatted for a few more minutes. "I better go. Ray is hovering over me now," Dot laughed.

After Gloria hung up, she grabbed her cell phone off the table and plopped her reading glasses on her nose. Paul had called.

She hadn't talked to Paul since the day before. It seemed as if so much had happened since then.

She called him back and he picked up right away. She explained the situation with Jill's offer on the house. When she tried to tell him about Dot, she could barely form a coherent sentence.

Finally, she burst into tears and began to sob. Paul tried his best to soothe his soon-to-be-bride over the phone and vowed that he needed to be around more and work less. Maybe it was time to set a firm retirement date.

Life was too short. What if Gloria had called to tell him she had cancer? Paul vowed that when he hung up, he would put in his notice. His last day would be December 31st.

It was time to start a new life with his new wife!

Gloria's sobs eventually turned to sniffles. She blew her nose loudly. "I'm sorry. I didn't mean to fall apart."

Paul assured Gloria she could cry anytime she needed to, as long as he wasn't the reason for her tears. "At least you got it out of your system before you see her tomorrow," he pointed out.

True. Gloria hadn't thought about that. She needed to show a brave face for her friend!

"It sounds as if your morning is booked," he said. "What if I come over on my next night off and we can talk more about the wedding."

So far, Paul had been content to leave all the planning to Gloria. His main priority was to make sure the two of them made it to the altar. Gloria and her friends could handle the rest.

"That sounds perfect," Gloria said. "I'll cook something special." She had no idea what that would be, but she had all evening to decide.

"No, I'll take you to dinner," he insisted, "somewhere nice."

After Gloria hung up the phone, she slid into the chair and pulled her lukewarm meal towards her. She picked up her fork and toyed with the food, her mind was a million miles away and her appetite had vanished.

Gloria managed to eat half of what was on her plate. She cut the rest of the meat into small pieces and split it between Mally and Puddles.

Gloria watched a little TV and then headed to bathroom to get ready for bed. Her body went through the motions as she brushed her teeth and washed her face.

She turned off the light and shuffled to the bedroom. If she herself felt this awful about

Dot's cancer, she couldn't even begin to imagine how her friend felt!

Chapter 8

Gloria's eyes popped open bright and early the next morning. It had taken a long time before she was finally able to drift off to sleep. When she did, she had jumbled dreams. In one of them, Dot was sprawled out on a stretcher, her hair tucked under a surgical cap as nurses wheeled her down a long hospital corridor.

Gloria chased after the stretcher and begged the nurses not to take her away, certain that she would never see her friend again.

There had been other dreams, but nothing as frightening as the one she remembered.

Mally was waiting at the door when Gloria wandered into the kitchen. She patiently stood by the door as Gloria fixed a pot of coffee. The coffee started to brew while she stepped out onto the porch.

A light frost covered the ground. The air was crisp and she watched as puffs of warm air escaped her lips. "Winter is right around the corner, girl," she told Mally.

Mally didn't care about winter – or snow. She was more concerned about patrolling the perimeter of the yard.

Thanksgiving was a few short weeks away. Gloria had been so focused on the upcoming visit from all of her children, not to mention the wedding; she hadn't had time to think about Turkey Day.

The coffee finished brewing. Gloria headed back inside to grab a cup from the cupboard and fill it.

Gloria grabbed her Bible and settled into a chair at the kitchen table. Morning Prayer and Bible reading was Gloria's favorite time of the day. The peace and quiet of the morning helped her to focus on the Word of God.

Not today, though. Her mind wandered. The ticking of the kitchen clock echoed in the room and the house creaked even more than usual, at least in Gloria's mind.

She made it through Psalm 104 and then closed her Bible. She meditated on the words and pushed back the chair from the table. It was time to get ready. It was time to solve the mystery of the house at 726 Pine Place!

***

Gloria pulled in Dot's drive and parked behind her van. She hadn't even had time to honk the horn when Dot sprang through the front door and down the cement steps.

Gloria studied her friend's face through the car window as she made her way to the passenger side. She looked...well, she looked at peace!

Dot pulled the door open and climbed in. She dropped her purse on the floor and reached for her seat belt. "I was up half the night."

Gloria reached over and patted Dot's arm. "I'm sorry, Dot. I had hoped you were able to get more rest than the night before."

Dot buckled the belt and adjusted the strap. "Believe it or not, I wasn't awake worrying about the you-know-what. I was thinking about Jill's house."

Gloria backed out of the drive and onto the road. "And?"

Two heads were better than one. Maybe Dot remembered something RJ had said that he forgot to mention to Gloria.

"Well, it seems to me that if the sellers keep insisting on large deposits and after they get the deposit, strange things start to happen, maybe it's a racket. You know, they keep making money on the place."

Gloria pulled to the stop sign and looked in both directions. "I was thinking the exact same thing. I mean, these aren't stellar, upstanding citizens in the first place, what with running a puppy mill."

"Maybe you could have Paul run a background check on them," Dot suggested.

Gloria raised a brow. "Great idea. I'll look into that."

The girls chatted about the restaurant, the upcoming holidays and Gloria's wedding. Gloria was careful to avoid mentioning doctors and surgery.

If, and when, Dot wanted to talk about it, she would.

Gloria pulled into the Highland Park neighborhood and turned onto Pine Place. The *For Sale* sign was still in the front yard. The real estate agent had taken down the top section, the part of the sign that read, *pending*.

She frowned. As far as she knew, it was still technically pending as long as the contract hadn't been cancelled!

Gloria shut off the engine and the girls climbed out of the car. She had gotten the access code for the lockbox from Jill. She punched in the code and removed the box cover.

The key fit the top lock. Gloria pushed the door open and waited for Dot to step inside. Dot followed Gloria through the living room and into the kitchen.

There was an odd odor in the house. Dot noticed it, too. She sniffed the air. "You smell that?" She wrinkled her nose.

Gloria waved a hand across her face. "Yuck! It smells like something died."

They walked through the house, checking cupboards and opening closet doors.

Gloria opened the dining room slider and the girls stepped onto the deck. "I don't get it. Unless the smell is coming from the attic."

After they cleared their lungs, they stepped back inside and Gloria closed and locked the slider. The girls checked each of the rooms and the lower level. The smell was definitely coming from somewhere upstairs.

They climbed the steps and walked back through the living room as they headed out the front door.

Dot grabbed Gloria's arm. She pointed to the living room fireplace. "We didn't check that."

They walked over to the beautiful, fieldstone fireplace. The odor grew stronger the closer they got to the mantle.

Dot pinched her nose and took short shallow breaths through her mouth. "It has to be coming from there."

Gloria was almost afraid to move the fireplace screen. Jill's sad face swam in front of her eyes. She was doing this for Jill, she reminded herself.

Gloria stuck her hand on the top of the decorative screen and lifted it up.

Dot gasped.

Gloria took a step back.

Curled up in a ball on top of the grate was a small, white bunny rabbit, its neck slashed. As much as Gloria wanted to drop the screen and run away, she took a step closer. She noticed several fresh puddles of blood. . The rabbit hadn't been there long.

Whoever killed the poor thing had done it recently. Brown streaks covered the fireplace insert, which Gloria surmised, was where the foul odor was coming from. The rabbit had not begun to smell. Whatever was in the insert smelled horrible!

Gloria fumbled inside her purse and pulled out her cell phone. She turned the screen to camera mode and snapped several pictures.

She replaced the metal screen and the girls made their way outside. "Should you tell the agent?"

Gloria nodded. "Yes, but we need to try to talk to the neighbors first."

Her head swung around as she looked at the neighbor's house on the left. A car was in the drive. There were also cars parked in the drive of the neighbor on the other side and the one across the street.

Gloria nodded to the right. "Let's start there."

She marched across the lawn and up the front steps of the house next door. Dot pushed the doorbell and the girls waited.

Moments later, the door slowly opened and a woman's face peered out. "Hi."

"Hello. My daughter has put an offer on the house next door and I wondered if I could ask you a couple questions." There was no need to beat around the bush.

The door opened wider. The woman, appearing to be in her early 30's with straight brown hair and sharp green eyes peered at them. "I wouldn't live in that house."

Dot leaned in. "Why not?"

"Because it's haunted."

Chapter 9

Gloria felt a momentary burst of disappointment. If Jill even heard a whisper of the word "haunted" there was no way she would live in the house. "Why do you think it's haunted?"

"The Acostas had a heck of a time...odd phone calls in the middle of the night, creaking noises coming from the attic, not to mention dead animals showing up on the doorstep." The woman shivered. "The last straw was when they came home one day and someone had drawn a pentagram on the dining room wall."

"I wouldn't live there, either," Dot declared. She turned to Gloria. "Maybe this isn't such a good idea."

Gloria frowned. Someone had scared the Acostas off...maybe even a neighbor.

"How long did the Acostas live in the house?" Gloria was curious.

The woman tapped the side of her cheek with her index finger. "Let me see. It had to have been a couple years. They moved in not long after my husband and I bought this place."

Dot knew where Gloria's questioning was headed. "They stayed in the house for two years even though it was haunted?"

The woman shook her head. "No. It was only the last few months that strange things started to happen."

Gloria thanked the woman for her time and Dot and she headed across the lawn. They stopped behind Annabelle.

Dot nodded at the place. "What do you think?"

"That it's mighty suspicious the house 'suddenly' became haunted."

Dot finished the sentence. "After having lived there for at least a year."

Gloria grabbed her arm. "C'mon. Let's talk to the people across the street."

They started down the drive at the same time the garage door on the house across the street opened. The occupant spotted the girls headed his way. It looked as if he planned to dart back in the house, the door half open. Gloria could hear a dog bark from somewhere inside.

Instead, he changed his mind as he shut the door and waited while they walked up the drive. "You the new neighbors? I heard they finally sold the house across the street."

Gloria shook her head. "My daughter and son-in-law have a contract on the house."

The man, short and thick with a few sparse hairs sticking out from under a ball cap, nodded. "The place has been empty for a while now. Is she sure she wants to live there?"

"The home is a good deal," Gloria pressed. "One of the neighbors said strange things started happening not long ago."

"True," he admitted. "Good riddance to the Acostas. They were an odd bunch."

He shoved his hands in his pockets. "They ran a puppy mill over there."

"So you didn't know them that well?" Dot piped up.

The man shook his head. "Nope. Only what the Holts told me." He pointed to the house Dot and Gloria had just left.

"Did the Acostas put the house up for sale and then odd things began to happen?"

"Not sure. Like I said, I wasn't real friendly with them." He rocked back on his heels. "I do know it wasn't long after the fire."

Gloria's eyes widened. "There was a fire?" Sue Camp had never mentioned a fire. Could it be the Acostas tried to burn the place down and collect on the insurance?

He shrugged. "Guess it was a small one. Fire department had it under control right away. Not a day or two later, the for-sale sign went up in the yard. The Acostas moved out quick. One day they lived there, the next day they were gone. I never saw a moving truck or anything."

The door leading into the house opened and a head popped out. "Ron, you've got a call."

The man excused himself. "I need to go. Sorry I couldn't be of more help." He turned on his heel and started up the steps.

The girls watched him go. "Maybe Jill doesn't want this house," Gloria said.

They had one more house to visit – the one on the other side. It was a large two-story with a spacious, covered porch.

Gloria admired the white wicker rocking chairs as they made their way to the front door.

Maybe once her remodeling projects were over, she would splurge and get new porch chairs.

The *thump, thump* of loud music echoed through the closed door. Gloria pressed the doorbell and waited. No one answered.

She tried again but there was still no answer.

"Maybe they can't hear the doorbell," Dot pointed out.

That was probably true. As loud as the music was through the closed door, Gloria could just imagine how much louder it was inside.

The girls finally gave up and headed back to the car. Gloria climbed into the driver's seat and slipped the key in the ignition. She was torn on whether or not she should call the real estate agent. She wasn't sure how happy Sue Camp would be if she found out Gloria had been inside the house.

She decided not to call. Sue Camp would find the poor, unfortunate bunny rabbit soon enough.

The girls rode for several long moments in silence. Before Gloria had left that morning, she had gotten the Acostas current address from Jill. The address was on the first page of the offer to buy the house.

She turned to Dot. "Do you have time to make a drive by the Acosta's new residence?"

"You thought of everything." Dot grinned. "Yeah. Sure. I have all day."

Gloria entered the address in her GPS and the girls were on their way. The address was still Rapid Creek but it wasn't in town. They drove past downtown and headed out into the country.

They passed several large farms before they reached their destination – a ramshackle, wood framed house with peeling paint and a sagging front porch. The house suffered from severe neglect. Several cars sat parked in the rutted drive. One car, minus the wheels, was sitting on carjacks and next to a long, narrow shed.

Gloria slowed the car but didn't stop.

Dot pointed out the window. "I see a dog run out back."

Gloria drove a mile down the road before she turned around for a second drive by. She was able to see a dog run and a dog kennel. "You think they're still selling dogs?"

Dot frowned. "It looks like it."

Short of stopping in the drive and knocking on the door, there wasn't much else to see. The house that the Acostas had moved out of was a lot nicer than the house they now lived in. If they were trying to swindle potential buyers out of their earnest money deposits, they certainly weren't spending the money on the house they currently lived in!

Gloria's heart sank. There wasn't much else to do except go home. Unless...

She jerked the wheel and careened into the driveway. "I have an idea."

Dot took a deep breath. "Oh no," she muttered. When Gloria had an idea, it could be a good thing...or it could be leading them right into a sticky situation. Based on the look on Gloria's face, Dot was leaning towards the sticky situation.

Gloria put the car in park, hopped out of the car and waded through the weed-infested lawn.

Not wanting to leave her friend in the lurch, Dot took a deep breath and opened the passenger side door. *Dear God, please protect us from whatever Gloria is about to get us into!*

By the time Dot caught up with Gloria, she had already knocked on the side door. "Just go along with whatever I say," Gloria mumbled under her breath.

"Got it."

The door creaked open a crack and a young face peered through the small opening. "Yes, ma'am."

"Hi...Uh...my friend and I," Gloria motioned to Dot, "heard that you might have some puppies for sale."

The door opened further, which was a good sign.

"I live alone and I'm looking for a new companion," Gloria blurted out. Mally would be thrilled – not!

The door swung open. The young woman, who couldn't have been more than sixteen years old, faced them. She wore a pair of ragged bib overalls and stained t-shirt. Her feet were bare. She eyed them with suspicion. "How'd you hear that we have puppies?" she asked.

"Uh..."

Dot weaseled her way closer. "Over at the post office in Belhaven." She scratched the side of her cheek. "There was a small sign on the bulletin board."

The petite brunette shoved her hands into her front pockets and frowned. "My mom and dad aren't home. I can show you what we have…"

Gloria clasped her hands together. "Perfect. Can we take the puppy home?"

The girl slipped her feet into a pair of ratty tennis shoes and grabbed a sweater from the back of the kitchen chair. "Maybe," she answered noncommittally.

Gloria and Dot followed the girl out to the backyard and behind a large, gray shed. Chunks of red paint had flaked off and dotted the weeds that surrounded the structure.

Woof! Woof! The barking of excited dogs wafted from inside the shed.

They rounded the corner and peeked inside the open door. Gloria's heart plummeted at the sight!

Stacked in metal crates three and four high were puppies, some of them so small Gloria could barely see them.

Tears stung the back of her eyes at the sight.

Next to her, Dot drew a ragged breath.

Gloria squeezed her eyes shut. She wanted to take each and every one of the dogs home today! *Pull yourself together, Gloria. You can't help these poor animals if you lose it now!*

She opened her eyes and steeled a closer look at the cages. One in particular caught her eye. Inside the cage was a scrawny little puppy, curled up in the back corner. He looked at her with drooping eyes but never made a move. He let out a sigh and buried his head under his paw.

Gloria stepped closer.

"That's Jasper. He's part lab and part mutt so we're having a hard time finding a home. Most people want purebred."

Gloria slipped her index finger through the bars. The inside of the cage was filthy and smelled horrible. She wrinkled her nose. "Hey, Jasper," she coaxed.

Jasper opened an eye, gazed at Gloria and then closed his eye again, clearly depressed.

"I'd like to take Jasper." She spun around and faced the girl. "How much?" Not that it mattered.

The girl's eyes darted to the cage. She could tell that Gloria wanted the dog. She could probably name her price and the woman wouldn't bat an eye. Jessica couldn't do that, though. Jasper had a special place in her heart, too, and she knew this woman was Jasper's best shot at a better life.

She threw out the first number that came to mind. "Ninety five dollars."

"Sold!" Gloria reached inside her purse. Luckily, she had enough cash on hand. She handed the girl a hundred dollar bill and waited while she unlocked the cage. Jessica slid her hand under the pup and pulled him out.

Dot was on the other side of the cramped shed, peering into a lower cage. "What about this one?" She pointed to a larger dog, bursting at the seams, his fur pressed tight against the cage that was two sizes too small for a large dog as large as he was.

The girl placed Jasper in Gloria's open arms. He barely stirred. Gloria hoped it wasn't too late, that the dog was just sad and not about to die. It would break Gloria's heart!

"That's Odie." The girl unlocked the cage and Odie burst out. Or maybe it was more like exploded. He hit the cement floor with a thud, landing on all fours.

The girl shoved her hands in her back pockets. "He's a handful," she warned.

Dot bent down to pat Odie's head.

Jessica continued. "I found him wandering on the side of the road last week. My parents were mad when I brought him home."

Jessica bent forward and stroked Odie's back. "They told me that we can't keep him and that if someone didn't take him this week, he would have to go."

Gloria and Jasper stepped closer. "Go where?"

Jessica's eyes met Gloria's eyes and then lowered. "Not sure," Jessica mumbled.

Dot shot to her feet. "That settles it then. I'll take Odie home with me!"

Jessica scuffed the tip of her shoe on the bare concrete floor. "My parents will be furious if I don't charge you," she said.

Dot opened the clasp of her purse. "How much?"

The girl shrugged, unsure how much a stray she picked up off the side of the road was worth.

"Twenty five dollars?" She lifted her brow and gazed into Dot's eyes.

Dot fumbled inside her purse and pulled out a twenty and ten. She shoved the bills into the girl's open hand. "Keep the change."

Before the girl could change her mind, Dot and Gloria stepped out of the "kennel" for lack of a better word, and headed toward the car.

Gloria took one final glance behind her at all of the sad faces of animals that she couldn't rescue, at least not today.

Dot and Gloria gave the dogs a few moments to take a potty break and then gently set them both on the back seat.

At least Gloria gently placed Jasper on the back seat. Odie tromped back and forth across the seat as he tried to look out the rear windows.

Gloria slid into the driver's seat and turned to Dot. "You sure you can handle that one?"

Dot waved a hand dismissively. "Yeah! Piece of cake."

She snaked a hand behind her and patted Odie's head. "Ray won't mind. He'll probably be happy that I have something to take my mind off the other."

Gloria had been so caught up in the puppy mill, she had completely forgotten about Dot's cancer – and her daughter's house dilemma!

Gloria backed out of the drive and pulled onto the road. She glanced in the rearview mirror. "We have to do something about those poor animals."

Dot agreed. "I was thinking the same thing." She adjusted the seatbelt across her lap. "Do you think those people and the dogs have something to do with the strange messages and someone scaring off potential buyers from the house?"

Gloria had been wondering the same thing. It didn't make sense that the people would kill their own deal so-to-speak, although they were collecting large non-refundable deposits as soon as they had the signed paperwork.

Gloria narrowed her eyes. *What if the real estate agent, Sue Camp, was involved?* She wondered how much Sue Camp stood to gain each time a buyer cancelled a contract. If she didn't make any money off the canceled contract, what benefit would it be to her for the property to remain on the market?

Looking back, the woman had seemed in an awful big hurry to cancel the contract instead of trying to work it out so that Jill and Greg would follow through with the purchase of the home.

If she had more time, she would swing by the agent's office and question her face-to-face. She glanced in the rearview mirror. Right now, she had a more pressing matter. Getting her new pooch home and welcomed into the family!

Chapter 10

Gloria dropped Dot and Odie off first. Ray was already home, waiting for his wife, when Gloria pulled in the drive. If he was surprised that they had a new family member, he did a great job of hiding it.

He greeted Odie as if they'd been together forever. Gloria grinned as she watched the three of them disappear inside the house.

Dot turned back for a second, gave her friend a "thumbs up" and then closed the door behind her. Odie might be the best medicine for Dot...far better than doctors or surgery, at least as far as lifting her spirits and giving her something to focus on other than the "c" word.

Back at the farm, Gloria pulled Annabelle into the garage and made her way to the rear passenger door.

Jasper lifted an ear and opened one eye when Gloria reached for him. "C'mon Jasper. We're home. Your new home. It's time to meet Mally and Puddles," she cajoled.

Jasper rose up on wobbly legs and tottered toward Gloria. Could it be the poor thing had spent so much time inside the cage that his legs weren't strong? Gloria felt a surge of heat rush through her.

She lifted Jasper from the backseat and then carried him over to the grass. He stood still for a long moment as he looked around. Gloria tried to see the farm through his eyes. It must look foreign and so very different from anything he'd ever seen before!

Jasper lifted his head and sniffed the cool, fall air. He took a step forward and then stopped. His whole body shook, as if overwhelmed by it all.

Gloria dropped to her knees and patted his back. "Don't worry Jasper. You're safe now."

She ran her hand down his legs. As soon as they were in the house, she was going to call the vet and make an appointment!

Jasper, feeling a little more confident with Gloria next to him, took a few tentative steps as he tottered over to the big oak tree. Mally's favorite tree.

Gloria's eyes darted to the back door. She could see Mally's face pressed tight against the window. How would Mally react to Jasper?

Jasper and she wandered around the yard. The more Jasper explored, the more confident he became. He explored the front yard and sniffed around the edge of the garden before he came back to Gloria and settled in at her feet.

Apparently, he had enough exploring for now!

She lifted Jasper and tucked him into the crook of her arm. It was time for Jasper to meet the rest of the family!

Gloria unlocked the door and let herself into the kitchen, keeping a firm grip on Jasper. He began to tremble when he caught sight of Mally, who was ten times larger!

Mally paced back and forth, trying to get close to Jasper.

Gloria held the door. "Want to go out, girl?"

Mally hesitated, looking from the door to Jasper, then back to the door. The outdoors won out and Mally raced across the porch and over to her favorite tree.

While Mally was outside, Gloria set Jasper on the floor of the guest bedroom. "I'll be back in a minute," she promised. She quietly closed the door behind her.

Gloria stepped out onto the porch and watched as Mally stretched her legs and darted around the yard. She disappeared on the far side of the garden – or what was left of it – and returned to the porch, an ear of corn clenched between her teeth.

She dropped it on the floor near Gloria's feet and looked up with pleading eyes, as if to say, "I can keep this, right?"

Gloria patted her head. "Yeah, you can keep it...finders keepers, I guess."

Mally picked the ear of corn back up and made her way to the porch door.

Gloria opened the door and waited for Mally to wander back inside. She watched as Mally dropped the ear of corn in her box of toys and trotted right into the dining room.

Gloria knew she was looking for Jasper.

Puddles was already at the bedroom door, his nose sniffing the perimeter. He flopped down on the floor and playfully stuck his paw under the frame, as if waiting for Jasper to join in.

Gloria lowered her head and peeked through the crack. She could see two small paws and the tip of Jasper's nose.

Mally whined and lowered down. Now both of her pets were trying to get in. They didn't seem agitated, just curious.

Gloria's cell phone chirped. She left the pets at the door and grabbed her phone off the table. It was Lucy. "How did it go?"

"How did what go?" So much had happened; she wasn't sure what Lucy wanted to know.

"Did you find anything interesting in the house?"

Gloria placed the palm of her hand on her forehead and closed her eyes. "Did we ever." She eyed the bedroom door.

Mally was trying to nudge the door open with her nose.

Puddles was using his back feet to kick at the door.

"Are you busy?" she asked Lucy.

Her friend yawned. "Nope," she said.

"Can you come down? I might need a second set of hands," Gloria told her.

"Sure." Lucy didn't probe. It was hard telling what exactly Gloria had gotten herself into, but knowing her friend, if she said she needed an extra hand, it had to be good!

Lucy grabbed her keys off the hook by the door and her purse from the chair. "I'm on my way!"

Gloria kept one eye on the bedroom door and the other on the driveway. Lucy made it in record time and Gloria held the door while she stepped inside.

Lucy took one look at Gloria's face and frowned. "Uh-oh. Something big happened." She dropped her purse on the table and shoved her keys in the side pocket. "Why do I always miss the good stuff?" she groaned.

"Woof!"

Jasper had finally found his voice, although it was more of a yap and less of a bark.

Lucy tilted her head and peeked into the dining room. "That wasn't Mally, unless she lost her voice."

"Nope." Gloria shook her head. "That was Jasper," Gloria said.

"Jasper?" Lucy started for the dining room. "You didn't..."

Gloria was right on her heels. "Oh, I did and so did Dot."

Lucy tiptoed past Gloria's pets, still firmly planted in front of the door. "Jasper is in here?" She tapped the outside of the bedroom door.

"Yep. Somehow, we need to get Puddles, Mally and Jasper acquainted. I figured it would be easier if I had a little help."

Lucy snorted. "Whatever possessed you to get another dog?" She held up her hand. "Wait! I'm sure this will involve more than a couple minutes explanation. Let's wait 'til the current crisis is over."

Gloria sucked in a breath and nodded. "Good idea."

She reached for Mally's collar and led her out to the kitchen. Lucy picked Puddles up and they trailed behind.

Gloria placed the doggie gate in the doorway that separated the kitchen from the dining room. Next, Lucy and she headed back to the guest bedroom.

Gloria opened the door and peeked around the corner. Jasper sat on the floor nearby. His ears drooped as he looked at Gloria then Lucy.

"Oh! How adorable!" Lucy reached out to pet his black fur.

He shrank back and began to quiver.

Lucy pulled her hand away. "He's terrified!"

Normally, Lucy was afraid of dogs. The only two dogs that her friend wasn't afraid to be around were Mally and Andrea's dog, Brutus. When Lucy was young, a dog had attacked her on her way home from school. She had ended up in the emergency room with several stitches on both of her arms and legs.

She had a fear of dogs...not the other way around. Lucy's heart melted. She dropped to the floor and crossed her legs. She patted the floor. "C'mere Jasper." She looked at Gloria. "Where did you get him?"

"It's a long story. A puppy mill."

Lucy shot her a look of surprise. It wasn't like Gloria to shop for a dog at a known puppy mill!

Gloria sighed. "Let's just say that I rescued Jasper and Dot rescued another dog, Odie."

Jasper tiptoed towards Lucy's outstretched hand then rubbed the top of his head on the palm of her hand.

"He likes you," Gloria said.

Lucy didn't move a muscle as Jasper sniffed her hand and then licked her thumb. After giving her the once-over, Jasper climbed onto Lucy's lap and curled into a ball.

Gloria clasped her hands together. "That dog belongs with you!"

Lucy stroked the top of Jasper's head. "I never thought I would say this, but I think you're right. He just stole my heart."

She rubbed his ear. "He's still trembling - just a little."

Her head shot up. "But you picked him out."

Gloria grinned. "I may have picked *him* out, but he most definitely picked *you* out!"

She knew right then and there that the matter was settled. Lucy, for the first time in her life, had a pet!

"Woof!" That bark belonged to Mally and Gloria could tell from the tone that her beloved pooch was getting anxious.

Lucy snuggled Jasper to her chest and carried him out of the bedroom.

Gloria stepped into the kitchen first. She bent down to Mally-level. "Don't you dare scare poor Jasper," she warned her. She turned to Puddles. "You, either."

Lucy stepped over the gate. Jasper eyed Mally, a look of sheer terror on his small face. "Maybe we should save the introductions for another day."

"I agree." Gloria opened the porch door and Lucy and Jasper stepped onto the porch.

Mally attempted to follow behind but Gloria stopped her. "Maybe next time, girl." Mally hadn't shown any sign of aggression but Jasper was too skittish and she didn't want the poor dog, who had probably already gone through so much, to be traumatized.

Lucy eased into the porch chair and settled Jasper onto her lap while Gloria slid into the other rocker. She explained everything that had happened up until the moment she called Lucy and asked her to come over.

Lucy rubbed Jasper's chin thoughtfully. "You mean there are more dogs, just like Jasper?"

Gloria nodded grimly. "A lot more. Somehow, some way, those poor animals need to be rescued."

Chapter 11

Gloria packed a goodie bag for Jasper, including some of Mally's favorite doggie treats. She gave Lucy the name and phone number of Mally and Puddles' vet, Andy Cohen, and then watched as Lucy loaded her new best bud in the front of the jeep and drove off.

Gloria couldn't have picked a better dog for her best friend if she tried.

She turned back to catch a glimpse of Mally's forlorn face in the window. She looked disappointed that Jasper was gone.

The Lord sure knew how to work things. Gloria already had her plate full, what with trying to plan the wedding, prepare for her kids holiday homecoming, solve the mystery surrounding Jill's house and now figure out how to rescue those poor pooches, not to mention deal with Dot's cancer.

Just the thought of all of that made her head spin. She glanced up at the skies. Clouds had started to gather but there were still several hours of daylight left. A nice, long walk back to the woods would do wonders and it would definitely cheer Mally.

She opened the kitchen door and stuck her head inside. "Want to go for a walk?"

Mally thumped her tail against the door and pushed past Gloria as she trotted out onto the porch.

Gloria grabbed her cell phone, a lightweight jacket from the hook and her house keys. She locked the door behind her but left all the lights on.

Mally darted ahead of Gloria, the path so familiar the two of them could probably make it back there with their eyes closed.

She stepped off the porch and glanced across the street at the small farm. The farm had once belonged to James and his family. James' grandparents had lived there for many years.

When they passed on, James' brother, who had never married, lived there for years until one day, he up and moved away after having met some woman on the internet. The last time Gloria had talked to him; he had married the woman and was now living somewhere in Minnesota.

The house sat vacant for several years before James finally sold it. He split the money from the sale evenly amongst the siblings. Local farmers had purchased the property, but only for the farmland. No one had ever moved into the house.

The empty house hadn't bothered Gloria. She rather liked the fact there was no one directly across the street. It appeared that was all about to change. Over the last few days, Gloria had noticed strange cars parked in the drive. She had even caught a glimpse of a young couple with a baby.

Gloria had a sneaking suspicion that the farmers had sold the house, which meant that soon she would have new neighbors.

For now, the house was empty, except for a dim light that shone through the front window, which is what caught Gloria's attention. There hadn't been any lights on in that house for years. Maybe whoever had bought it had left an interior light on by accident.

She shrugged her shoulders and turned her attention to more pressing things.

Halfway across the backfield, Gloria's cell phone rang. It was Paul. "How's my girl?"

"Overwhelmed," Gloria admitted. The cell reception was good and Paul was coming in loud and clear.

"Did you find anything out about Jill's place?" he asked.

Gloria told him how her day had gone and ended with Lucy taking Jasper home with her. "So I dodged another dog?" he teased.

"So far," Gloria admitted. "There are more that need to be rescued."

She knew there was no way she could take all of those dogs. Even if she convinced every single one of her friends to adopt one of the dogs, there would still be too many. She couldn't just set them free. That was irresponsible.

On top of that, what would stop the Acostas from going out and getting more to replace the ones they had sold?

No. There had to be another plan...a better one. She needed to find out more about the people who ran the mill – Jessica's parents. She could send someone else over there to sort of scope the place out, maybe glean a little more information into the Acosta's background and in the process find out more about Jill's place!

137

"...so we could honeymoon on Mackinac Island."

Paul was talking. Gloria hadn't heard a word he had said, although she caught the tail end. "That would be lovely," she replied.

Paul snorted. "You didn't hear a word I said, did you?"

"Only the part about Mackinac Island," she admitted. "I love that place."

"We can't honeymoon there in the middle of winter, unless you plan on getting there by snowmobile," he pointed out.

That was true. The island was somewhat remote, accessible only by boat or small plane. In the winter, the only way to get there was by snowmobile. Visions of Gloria in an elegant, lacy dress wearing snowmobile boots, snow pants and a ski jacket filled her head.

"Maybe we should go somewhere warm and save that for next summer," she suggested.

She changed the subject. "About that puppy mill. Aren't those illegal?" she asked.

Paul paused. "Not that I know of...at least not if they're registered."

"Can you find out?" she asked.

"I'll see what I can do," he promised. "Are you too busy with all of your dilemmas to have dinner with your betrothed?" he teased.

She was in the woods now and had settled onto her favorite log. "Of course not."

"Good. I can't make it tomorrow but I have the next night off. Maybe we can have dinner at that Italian place you investigated not long ago over in Lakeville...what was the name?"

"Pasta Amore." Gloria was surprised she remembered, what with all the stuff running through her head.

"Yes, dinner at Pasta Amore," he agreed.

After Gloria finished talking to Paul, she wandered over to the edge of the creek. The water level had dropped. Fall had been dry but winter was on the way and it would fill back up during the winter season and when the snow melted in the spring.

She glanced around the woods that she loved. The place had brought her many hours of quiet reflection when she needed to be by herself and clear her mind. She wondered if this would be her last visit before Paul and she married and if Paul would come here with her, too.

On the one hand, she wanted to share it with him, but on the other, it was her own secret hideaway. She guessed she would have to start sharing some things.

Mally had finished splashing in the creek and raced over to Gloria. "Ready to head back, Mally?"

Mally circled her several times and then raced ahead to the edge of the woods.

The light on her answering machine was blinking when Gloria stepped back inside the kitchen. She hung her jacket on the hook near the door, stepped to the kitchen counter and pressed the button on the machine. It was Jill.

"Hey Mom. It's me." She let out a heavy sigh. "I called to find out if you came up with anything on the house. It looks like we didn't get the house we put an offer in on yesterday. The owners went with another offer so we are once again homeless."

Gloria could hear the frustration in her daughter's voice. "Anyways, call me back. Thanks."

Gloria promptly dialed her daughter's number. Tyler answered. "Hi Grams. Mom said we might be moving in with you."

A stab of sheer something ran through Gloria. She had offered to let Jill, Greg and the boys live with her if they needed to, but she hadn't seriously pondered the idea.

141

If Gloria couldn't figure out who was trying to stop them from purchasing the house on Pine Place, they may very well have to move in with Gloria – lock, stock and barrel!

She had visions of Paul, her kids and her grandkids all living under one roof. She wondered if perhaps she could just run away.

She grinned as she envisioned dragging her suitcase out of the house...peeling out of the driveway in Annabelle as if the devil himself were on her heels.

He went on. "Ryan and I already decided that we're gonna live in the tree fort." Well, that solved some of the crowding issues!

Gloria swallowed the lump in her throat. "That's quite a thought, Tyler," she said. "Is your mom there?"

Tyler handed the phone to his mother.

"Sorry Mom. You know that would be a last resort," she assured her. "Did you find anything out about the house?"

"Not much...yet," Gloria admitted. "I'm still working through some of the clues and will be on it first thing in the morning," she vowed. *With a vengeance,* she silently added.

"We have a couple houses to look at tonight, but I can already tell that they won't work. They're either in the wrong school district, the yard is too small or the price is too high."

Perhaps Gloria could add a little more cash for the purchase. Desperate times called for desperate measures. "I may be able to give you more money if you're close on price," Gloria told her.

Jill stopped her. "No! We aren't going to do that. First of all, it wouldn't be fair to give me more money than Eddie and Ben got and second of all, you've already been far too generous."

Jill had a point. If Gloria gave her daughter more money, it would only be right to give her sons more, too. "Well, don't give up on that house yet, Jill. I haven't failed to crack a case yet."

Jill sighed. "True. If ever there was a time I needed you to get to the bottom of something, now is it!"

Gloria reassured her daughter it was a top priority and hung up the phone. She stared at the silent phone in her hand and closed her eyes. "Dear God. Please help me figure out who is trying to stop Jill from buying that home."

She lifted her head and gazed out the window. Gloria needed help and fast. There was only one place to go.

She grabbed her purse from the table, the keys from the hook by the door and headed to Dot's Restaurant.

She swung by Lucy's place on the way. Lucy met her at the door. "Where are you going?"

"Dot's Restaurant. I need some help on Jill's house." She told her about her conversation with Jill.

Lucy scrunched her nose. "Wow! Yeah, this is a 911 emergency, for sure. Let me get my purse."

Gloria stood at the door and waited. Jasper wandered over, his tail wagging. He looked different, somehow...happy. She bent down and kissed his head. He smelled fresh, like lemons.

Lucy was back.

Gloria looked up. "Did you give Jasper a bath already?"

Lucy laughed. "Yep. He loves baths. He had a ball."

"Woof!" Jasper turned adoring eyes to Lucy.

"I'll be back before you know it," she promised her pooch.

Two sad, brown eyes bore into Lucy's own. "Ugh! Don't look at me like that!"

Gloria grinned. "Better get used to it. I call it the pitiful play. Don't worry, he'll be thrilled when you return and completely forget that you left him at home."

Lucy glanced down at Jasper one final time. "I hope you're right," she fretted.

The girls discussed the house on the way to Dot's place. This one had Gloria stumped, something she'd never had happen before. She always had an idea on how to solve a mystery, but this time her mind was blank.

"Maybe you have too much going on," Lucy pointed out.

Wasn't that the truth! The house, Dot's cancer, the puppy mill, the wedding and the holidays was so much! Her head was spinning just trying to organize the events. Now she had to wonder if Jill and her family were going to have to move in.

Soon, she would be ready for the nut house. It wasn't that she didn't love them all to pieces, but there was only so much one person could take!

"You can come stay with me," Lucy offered.

Gloria pulled Annabelle into an open spot in front of the restaurant and shut the engine off. "I may take you up on that...seriously."

Dot's Restaurant was busy but not packed. Gloria caught a glimpse of Margaret and her husband, Don, in a booth in the back.

Dot was standing near their table, coffee pot in hand.

Gloria pointed at the pot. "You're not supposed to be here," she accused her friend.

Dot lifted a hand. "I can't help it. What am I supposed to do? Sit home and twiddle my thumbs, worrying that the cancer cells are multiplying?"

True. Dot had a point. If Gloria were in the same position, she wasn't sure that she would be able to sit still.

She changed the subject. "How is Odie adjusting?"

Dot pointed a finger toward the kitchen. "He's great! He's in the back, helping Ray." She leaned forward. "He loves that dog!"

Gloria was relieved. She felt responsible for dragging Dot along to the puppy mill in the first place.

"How is Jasper?" Dot asked.

Lucy settled into the chair next to Margaret. "He's adjusting quite nicely."

Dot raised a brow. "Really?"

"Lucy came over to help me with the dogs and Jasper took a liking to her," Gloria explained.

"Huh." Dot shoved a hand on her hip. "Lucy has a dog. Miracles never cease."

"What miracle?" Ruth had come up behind Gloria and now stood near the table. She shrugged out of her jacket and dropped it on the back of the chair.

"Lucy has a dog," Dot explained.

Ruth raised a brow. "Lucy? Our Lucy?"

"We can tease Lucy later." Gloria changed the subject. "I need all of your help and fast!"

Chapter 12

Gloria outlined her dilemma. The girls clucked in sympathy when she got to the part where she feared her entire family would be moving in, lock stock and barrel. "So I need to figure out what in the world is going on at that house and fast!" she finished.

Dot had returned with several cups of coffee and a small pot of hot water and packet of hot chocolate for Lucy.

Lucy dumped the packet in the bottom of the empty cup then poured hot water over the top. She stirred the mix and took a sip. Her face puckered. "I think they stopped putting sugar in this stuff."

She reached for several sugar packets, tore the ends off three and dumped them into her cup. She stirred the contents and took a sip. "Much better," she decided.

Her gaze turned to Gloria. "What about another stakeout?"

"But what would we stake out? The house is empty," Ruth pointed out.

Margaret snapped her fingers. "What about the real estate agent? She must know something more that she hasn't shared."

Gloria suspected the same...that Sue Camp knew more than she was letting on. "I'll track her down in the morning."

Dot returned. "Follow the money." She refilled the girls' cups and set the carafe on the edge of the table.

Gloria looked up. Her eyes narrowed. "Follow the money and find out who cashed in the previous earnest money deposits."

She patted Dot's hand. "Great idea. Why didn't I think of that?"

"Love has clouded your head," Lucy joked.

"That, or fear," Ruth added.

After Gloria and Lucy finished eating, they climbed back in the car. Lucy was carrying a small folded napkin.

Gloria pointed at her lap. "Whatcha got in there?"

Lucy's eyes fell to her lap. "Just a little snack for Jasper."

"Hm." Gloria smiled knowingly. Yep. The dog had officially taken over and now controlled Lucy's life. She hoped that Max liked dogs...

Back at Lucy's ranch, Gloria waited for her friend to make her way inside before she pulled out of the driveway and headed home. She would need to get a good night's rest. She wanted to be up early the next morning to corner Sue Camp in her office!

***

Gloria, feeling guilty that she had left Mally at home the last few trips from the farm, decided to bring her sidekick along. Mally was happy as a clam to be in the car and going somewhere – anywhere!

Green Springs Premier Realty's parking lot was almost empty, except for two cars. She hoped that one of the cars belonged to Sue Camp.

Gloria slid out of the driver's seat. "I'll be right back," she told Mally. She wasn't sure if they allowed dogs in the office and she didn't want to give Sue Camp a single excuse for not talking to her.

The front office door was unlocked. Gloria turned the knob and stepped inside. A young woman sat at the front desk, filing her fingernails. She looked up when Gloria closed the door behind her.

"Can I help you?"

"Yes, I'm looking for Sue Camp."

The girl's eyes darted to the back of the building. "Let me see if she's in."

Gloria smiled. "Thank you."

The girl slid out of the seat and scurried down the hall and out of sight.

The girl returned a few moments later. "She is here and will be right with you."

Gloria nodded, then turned her attention to the bulletin board, chock full of houses for sale.

Moments later, a surprised Sue Camp wandered into the reception area. "Oh! Hello Mrs. Rutherford. What brings you to my office bright and early this morning? Looking for a new home?"

Sue Camp had heard the gossip. She knew that her client's mother had given her money to purchase a new home.

"I'm sure that my daughter, Jill, told you that as of right now, they are still moving forward on the purchase of 726 Pine Place."

The woman rested her hip against the counter. "Are you sure? I mean, that house has her a little rattled what with the mysterious notes and such."

Gloria pulled her purse in front of her and leveled her gaze. "Why do you think those things are happening, Ms. Camp?"

The woman shrugged. "I wouldn't have the slightest idea."

Gloria took a step forward. "None whatsoever?"

The woman was nervous. Gloria could smell it from a mile away. "Who keeps the deposit money when a deal falls through?"

"Not me," she answered.

"The sellers?" Gloria probed.

"I don't know where you're going with all these questions." The woman's eyes narrowed. "Look! I have no idea who is trying to drive off buyers. All I know is that it's not me."

She turned on her heel and stomped into the back office, slamming the door behind her.

The girl behind the counter gasped. Her mouth fell open, then quickly closed. She promptly clamped it shut and picked up her nail file.

Gloria turned on her heel and slowly stepped out the front door. Something was going on and Gloria was determined to find out what!

She climbed behind the wheel of her car and headed to Rapid Creek. There was still one neighbor Gloria hadn't talked to; now was as good a time as any.

She pulled in the drive at 726 Pine Place and climbed out of the car. Still prominently displayed in the front yard was the "for sale" sign, minus the "pending" part.

Gloria stepped to the end of the drive and turned left, toward the two-story house next door. Once again, she heard the loud thump of rock music before she reached the door.

Someone had tossed a newspaper into the grass out front. Out of habit, Gloria reached over to pick it up. The yard was full of land mines. Big land mines. Whoever lived inside this house had a large dog - or two.

When she reached the front door, the music abruptly stopped. She raised her hand to ring the bell when the door swung open.

Behind the screen door stood a tall, gangly teen with ear buds draped around his neck. He had a tight grip on the collar of a large German Shepherd that looked none too happy to see Gloria. He bared his teeth, lowered his ears and let out a low warning growl.

Gloria glanced at the flimsy screen that separated them. If the dog wanted to, he could burst through the screen as if it wasn't even there.

"H-hi. My name is Gloria Rutherford and my daughter is buying the house next door." Gloria pointed to the house. "I was wondering if you could tell me about the neighbors...the Acostas who recently moved out."

The dog leaned forward and gave another warning growl.

She glanced at the dog. Maybe it wasn't such a good idea for Jill and the boys to move next door. What if the dog got loose and attacked one of her grandsons?

The first thing they would need was a fence. She made a mental note to discuss the matter with her daughter.

From a distance, somewhere in the back of the house, Gloria heard another bark. She could tell from the bark that it was a much smaller dog.

The boy shrugged. "Yeah, they moved out kinda fast. Like overnight. They had a ton of dogs out back."

"Did you ever see the dogs?" Gloria was curious.

"Yep. My mom and dad bought one before they moved."

The house phone began to ring. "I gotta go."

Before Gloria had a chance to reply, the boy closed the door in her face. She heard the lock turn. The large dog barked until Gloria was off the porch and back on the sidewalk.

She wandered around the side of the empty house and into the back yard. She hadn't noticed before, but the rear yard was partially fenced. Well, maybe partially wasn't quite accurate. There was a haphazard fence. Several boards were missing and it tilted at a precarious angle, as if a good, strong wind would knock it over.

She glanced over the top of the rickety fence and into the neighbor's yard. There was nothing to prevent the puppy mill dogs and the neighbor's dogs from wandering into each other's yards.

Obviously, the neighbors got along if what the boy said was true, that they had purchased a dog from the Acostas. What if they had purchased a dog and it had died?

Gloria needed to get someone back inside the puppy farm, to try to glean more information out of the owners and check on the dogs...

She also needed to set up some sort of surveillance at the house. Gloria stepped onto the back deck. She shaded her eyes and peered into the rear slider. She needed someone who could loan her some sort of surveillance equipment for a day or two...

Gloria took a step back. She knew just who to ask!

Chapter 13

Ruth Carpenter clicked the end of the ballpoint pen and studied Gloria. "So you need me to loan you my surveillance equipment?"

Gloria nodded. "It will only be for a couple days. I promise."

Ruth turned her gaze to the SP5500 Series spy camera she had recently purchased with the garage sale money she had made at Gloria's house. It was her prized possession...her baby. She used it every night after work.

Since the drug bust at the post office, things had been quiet, but Ruth knew that could change at any moment and nothing was ever gonna get by her again. Not on her watch!

"Okay, you can borrow it but only for a day or two," Ruth relented. "How soon?"

"Now?" Gloria knew Ruth wasn't big on having surprises sprung on her, especially when it involved her spy equipment.

Ruth frowned.

"I have a better idea." Gloria changed her mind. "Why don't we head over there after work tonight?"

It sounded perfect until Gloria remembered her date with Paul. "I mean, tomorrow night after work and you can help me set it up. You know, make sure it's installed correctly."

Gloria knew that would pacify Ruth somewhat, to know that no one would be handling the equipment except her.

"Okay. We can do that," Ruth agreed.

Gloria told Ruth she would pick her up at 5 o'clock sharp the next afternoon and then headed out of the post office.

Next on her list was finding someone to make a trip out to the Acosta's new place, pretending to be interested in a puppy. She had just the person for the job.

Gloria headed up the hill to Magnolia Mansion and Andrea's place.

***

Gloria pulled in the drive and rounded the small bend. Andrea's luxurious Mercedes sports car wasn't in the drive. In its place was a four-wheel drive pick-up truck. It looked new.

Gloria slid out of the car and slowly closed the car door.

Behind her, a construction crew was hard at work on the walls of Andrea's new detached garage.

Andrea had told her she wanted to have the garage finished before the first snowflake hit the ground. It looked like she was going to make that deadline.

Gloria eased past the pick-up truck. On closer inspection, the truck was a beautiful metallic dark blue color. From what she could tell, it was a roomy four door.

"Checking out my new ride?" Andrea called from the doorway. She didn't wait for Gloria to answer. She shoved her feet into a pair of clogs that sat just outside the door and shuffled over to the truck.

Andrea pressed the button on the clicker in her hand and unlocked the driver's side door. She grabbed the handle and swung the door open. "Hop in."

Gloria had, on and off, thought about buying a pick-up truck. It would come in handy during the winter months when snow blew across the flat farm fields creating large snowdrifts on the roads. There were days it was nearly impossible to get around during a snowstorm, not that Gloria liked to drive around in snowstorms in the first place!

She climbed into the driver seat and wiggled around on the leather seat. She reached over and rubbed the gray strip of cloth that covered the spacious center console.

Andrea smiled. "You can see pretty good from up there, huh?"

Andrea was right. Gloria could see a lot more in the truck than she could when she was behind the wheel of Annabelle. The seats were large and, for a truck, luxurious. This was no cheap run-of-the-mill truck. Gloria was certain Andrea had paid a pretty penny for it.

Gloria could afford to buy a new vehicle with her windfall, although it didn't seem like a necessity. Still, it would be nice to have something that got around in the winter better than her car.

She closed her eyes and breathed deeply. The smell of brand new vehicle filled her nose. It had been years since she'd been inside a new vehicle, let alone driven one.

Gloria eased out of the driver's seat and slid to the ground. "I'm sure this set you back a pretty penny."

Andrea nodded and then closed the driver's side door. "Yep." She shrugged. "The Mercedes wasn't practical, at least not living out here."

The girls made their way to the house. "You should think about getting one," she added.

Gloria grinned. She stopped in her tracks and turned back. "Nah, I can just call you to come pull me out of the ditch now," she teased.

The girls wandered inside. Alice, Andrea's new housemate and former housekeeper, met them in the hall. "You like Miss Andrea's new truck?"

Gloria smiled at the petite woman. "Yes. Are you going to drive it?" Now that Gloria thought about it, she wasn't sure if Alice knew how to drive.

Alice waved her hands in front of her. "No! No! Not me!"

Andrea patted Alice's arm. "Alice would like to learn how to drive but I'm afraid now that I have the truck, she thinks it's too big."

Gloria adjusted the purse on her shoulder. "Do you think Annabelle – my car- would be too big?"

Alice glanced uneasily over Gloria's shoulder, past Andrea's new truck at Gloria's car. "Well…"

"I-I think…" Alice said nervously.

Gloria interrupted. "Great. It's settled. We can start your first driving lesson today."

Gloria had enough on her plate, but what if there was an emergency and Andrea wasn't home – or worse yet – something happened and Alice needed to drive somewhere? At the very least, she should be able to get help!

Gloria could tell from the look on Alice's face that she was starting to waffle. "Go grab your purse."

Alice opened her mouth and then closed it. She turned on her heel and headed up the steps.

Andrea and Gloria watched until she disappeared from sight.

Andrea turned to Gloria, her eyes wide. "You're going to teach her to drive? I've been trying for weeks now to get her behind the wheel and she keeps coming up with excuses."

Gloria grinned. "No time like the present."

Alice returned a few moments later. The first thing Gloria noticed was her olive complexion was pale...just a tad. The second thing she noticed was that Alice's hand trembled as she nervously shifted the small handbag in her hand.

Gloria swung her arm around her shoulder. "You'll do fine."

The girls marched out the front door and over to Annabelle. Gloria clicked the key fob to unlock the doors and then opened the driver's side door. She waved her hand at Alice to slide into the driver's seat. "We'll start slow," she promised.

Alice swallowed the lump in her throat and nodded, too terrified to speak.

Andrea climbed in the back seat while Gloria made her way to the passenger side. When the women were safely inside the car, she told Alice to start the engine.

Two terror-filled eyes gazed at Gloria. "Now?"

Gloria nodded. "Yes. Now," she urged.

Alice started the car. She made a cross sign using her hand. "Protect us, Jesus."

Slowly, step-by-step, Gloria instructed Alice on how to back the car out of the drive. Alice took a very wide turn and only one of the construction workers had to dive for cover when she panicked and pressed the gas pedal instead of the brake.

They crept out onto the road. "Turn right," Gloria told her when they reached the end of the long, gravel drive.

The car, as if in slow motion, turned onto the road and started down the steep hill. It was a dead end road and it ended near a small public access beach and boat launch.

Alice turned the steering wheel and made a large swooping circle. The front bumper grazed one of the metal guardrails that lined the edge of the road as the car careened to the side.

Alice turned terrified eyes to Gloria. "I'm sorry!"

"Don't worry about it," Gloria assured her, "Annabelle is tough."

After the car was back in the drive, safely parked behind Andrea's new truck, Alice shut the engine off and dropped her forehead on the steering wheel.

Gloria patted Alice's back. "Great job, Alice!"

The woman lifted her head. "You think so, Miss Gloria?"

Andrea unbuckled her seatbelt and leaned forward in the seat. "Yes! Next time we can drive into downtown!"

Alice groaned and Gloria grinned.

The girls headed back inside the house. Brutus, Andrea's dog, waited by the door, as if wondering why he hadn't been invited for a ride. Gloria reached down and patted his head. "I'm sorry, Brutus. I plum forgot about you!"

The girls wandered into the kitchen. Andrea stepped over to the back counter and grabbed a coffee cup from the cupboard. "Coffee?"

Gloria nodded. "Yes, thanks."

Andrea poured a cup and set it in front of Gloria. "So what brings you by?"

Gloria wasn't one to show up unannounced, unless, of course, she had a specific reason. Andrea knew her friend well enough to know there was a reason.

"I have a favor to ask." She went on to explain everything that had happened and ended with: "Can you take a run by the Acosta's place and scope out the puppy mill?"

Gloria had done so much for Andrea, her friend could ask her to fly to the moon and she would tell her yes. "Of course," she replied.

Alice, who had settled in at the bar, sat silent.

Gloria turned to her. "Would you mind going with her?" she asked.

Alice brightened. So far, she had never been involved in one of Gloria's investigations. "Yes!"

Gloria slapped the palm of her hand on the gleaming counter. "Great! It's settled!"

Andrea jotted down the address and Gloria gave them instructions on where the puppy mill was located. She looked up from the notepad and frowned. "What do I say if they ask how I found them?"

Gloria gazed out the window thoughtfully. "Well, you can tell them that your friend came by the other day and Jessica helped them purchase two of the dogs. Maybe they will think they have another easy sale." Not that Andrea needed another dog...

"You don't have to take one of the dogs," Gloria went on, "tell them that you have to think about it."

Andrea nodded. "Sounds good." She changed the subject. "A little birdie told me you were thinking about having your wedding here at the house."

Gloria had almost forgotten! "Yeah. One of the girls suggested it."

Alice piped up. "Yes, Miss Gloria. That would be beautiful. I can prepare some of my famous Mexican dishes for the reception!"

Gloria loved Alice's spicy dishes but they didn't love her back. The last thing she needed to do was eat a bunch of spicy food on her wedding day. "Uh..."

Alice's firehouse fajitas + Gloria's wedding night = recipe for disaster!

Andrea patted Gloria's shoulder. "We will definitely have Alice's world famous fajitas but probably some other dishes to go along with them." She winked at Gloria who breathed a sigh of relief.

The last thing she wanted to do was to hurt Alice's feelings. "Great. Maybe we can go over some sort of menu."

"The wedding will be here before you know it," Andrea pointed out.

The way Gloria's life was going, ten weeks would fly right out the window and before she knew it, she would be walking down the aisle, or in the case, across the sunroom. "We can do a tentative menu now, if you want."

Andrea grabbed a notepad from the back counter and a pen from a small penholder nearby. The three women came up with the perfect menu. Not only would they have Alice's firehouse fajitas, they would include some dishes from Dot's restaurant: stick-to-your-ribs foods like baked chicken, sliced beef, mashed potatoes and macaroni and cheese.

"This won't be too much work for you?" Gloria asked.

Alice interrupted. "No, Miss Gloria. Andrea and I already talked about having my sister from Texas come help." She pronounced "sister" as "seestar" and Gloria smiled. "We will take care of everything."

Gloria tipped her head back and swallowed the last of her coffee. "When you come up with an estimate of how much it will cost, let me know and I'll write a check," she said gratefully.

She suddenly remembered Dot's cancer. What if Dot wasn't up to catering a wedding? They would need a back-up plan.

As Gloria explained Dot's situation, Andrea teared up. She reached for a Kleenex and dabbed her eyes. "Oh...I had no idea."

Gloria hadn't meant to upset Andrea. "We have to believe that the Lord is going to heal Dot."

Andrea nodded. "I'll add her to my prayers."

"Me too," Alice whispered. She didn't know Dot as well as some of the others, but any friend of Andrea's was a friend of hers.

Alice and Andrea walked Gloria to the front door. "We'll head over to the Acosta's place as soon as I shower," Andrea promised.

Gloria hugged them both and headed to her car. Things were falling into place.

Gloria's wheels were spinning on the way home. She needed to convince Jill to move forward with that house! Whoever was trying to scare them off would make another move soon and Gloria hoped to catch them in the act!

Now all she had to do was convince Jill.

Chapter 14

"Are you one hundred percent *sure*?" Jill asked.

"Yes, I am." Gloria had finally convinced her daughter to move forward on the ranch house at 726 Pine Place. "If something happens and you have to back out, I will replace the lost deposit AND you, Greg and the kids can stay at the farm until you find another house."

"I need you to call Sue Camp and tell her that you're bringing a home inspector through the house," Gloria added.

Gloria hung up the phone and twisted the engagement ring around her finger nervously. The pressure was on! If ever there was motivation to solve a mystery, this was it!

She spent the rest of the afternoon cleaning house. There were two bedrooms upstairs that the boys could use and then the guest bedroom downstairs where Greg and Jill could sleep.

Ben, Gloria's middle child, his wife Kelly and their twins, Ariel and Oliver, would be here a few days before Christmas. Their flight home was the day after Christmas.

Gloria's oldest child, her son, Eddie, and his wife, Karen, planned to come for the same days, but it was only the two of them.

Gloria mentally counted eleven people shacked up in a four-bedroom house. The adults could get the bedrooms and she could turn the living room into a huge sleepover for her grandchildren. The boys would outnumber poor Ariel. Gloria hadn't seen her granddaughter in almost a year now.

It would only be for a few days, she tried to convince herself. A few days to house her entire family, marry Paul and celebrate Christmas. The idea of getting married when everyone was in town had seemed like a brilliant plan at the time. Now she wasn't so sure.

Remain positive, she told herself. *We need to get Jill in that house, safe and sound!*

The afternoon flew by and Gloria had just enough time to take a bath and change into a clean outfit before Paul arrived.

Mally saw Paul first, her excited bark announcing his arrival. Gloria opened the door as he reached the top step. He was holding a bouquet of beautiful fall flowers. Gloria reached for the flowers and lifted up on her tippy toes at the same time for a kiss.

She closed her eyes and breathed in his cologne. Gloria loved the musky, masculine scent. For a moment, all was right in her world. Gone were thoughts of puppy mills and haunted houses.

Paul wrapped his arms around his bride-to-be and drew her close. "I've been waiting for this all day!"

Gloria laid her cheek on his chest and soaked it in, the flowers still clutched in her grip.

Finally, Paul backed up. "You are more beautiful each time I see you," he said.

Gloria blushed. "I bet you say that to all the girls," she shot back.

Paul bent down for a second kiss. "Only my girl," he promised.

Moments later, Gloria reluctantly stepped away as she headed to the cupboard. She reached inside and pulled out a large, glass vase. She filled the vase with water and set the flowers inside.

With a little arranging, the blooms filled the vase and spilled over the sides. "You're spoiling me," she said as she set the vase in the center of the kitchen table.

Paul pulled out a chair and sat down. "This is just the beginning," he assured her.

Paul was Gloria's perfect mate. He was her anchor. He had the patience of a saint...never annoyed with her when she got herself into a pickle, which she'd done on more than one occasion.

On top of all that, he was easygoing, which she chalked up to working as a police officer for decades. One would have to have a lot of patience for that line of work.

Gloria worried about him, though. He still patrolled the streets some nights. At least there wasn't a ton of serious crimes in Montbay County.

The last murder investigation had been the one that involved Andrea's place and the body they had stumbled upon had been decades old.

No, the crimes in the area were more along the lines of missing persons, drug activity... Now that

Gloria thought about it, she had been involved in several of those as well!

Still, she would be relieved when he retired, which would bring on a completely new set of worries. If he retired, would they get on each other's nerves? They would be newlyweds and with Gloria's windfall, maybe they could do a little traveling, find a new hobby that didn't involve dead bodies...

"Earth to Gloria," Paul said.

Gloria snapped to attention. "I'm sorry. I guess my mind had wandered."

"Let me guess. Your new investigation," he said.

"Kind of." She didn't want to admit she was nervous about married life. Instead, she told him the status of Jill's house.

He frowned. "You think there's a chance that they might have to move in with you?" Gloria was good at juggling a lot of different things at once, but all of this might be too much, especially with the wedding. The last thing hc needed was for her to become overwhelmed and get cold feet!

"If that happens, some of them can come stay at my place," he offered.

Gloria smiled at the generous offer. She didn't want to impose but it was a thought, especially if it got as crowded as she envisioned. "Thank you, but hopefully it doesn't come to that."

Paul didn't dare mention that his son, Jeff, and daughter-in-law, Tina, were having trouble paying their rent and had hinted at moving back in with him.

He glanced at the clock. "Ready to hit the road?" He stood, lifted his arms over his head and stretched his back. It had been a long week and this was the first chance he'd had to relax.

The restaurant, Pasta Amore, was in the nearby town of Lakeville. Gloria had eaten there a couple times. One time was with Paul and another time with the Garden Girls when they were investigating the deadly poisoning at Dot's Restaurant.

She couldn't remember much about the place, other than the food was delicious, but not as good as the food that Dot served.

During the drive, Gloria told him about the wedding plans and the menu that Andrea and she had discussed. He told her he would leave all of that up to her. All he needed to know was what time he had to be there.

Gloria was a "take charge" person and the fact that he left those details up to her suited her just fine.

Paul parked his truck in an empty space in front of the restaurant and climbed out of the driver's seat. Gloria knew date night meant she had to wait until he came around the other side and opened her door.

She put her hand in his and slid out of the truck. The last special date night had been when he had taken her on the dinner cruise over at Lake Harmony. If they had planned a summer wedding, Lake Harmony would have been the perfect spot to get hitched!

Paul held the door and Gloria stepped inside the dimly lit restaurant. It looked different than the last time she had been there. The setting was more intimate. Red-checkered tablecloths covered the tables. A small, flickering candle sat in the center of each of the tables.

The hostess stepped forward. "Table for two?"

Paul nodded. "Give us the most romantic one you've got."

"Of course." She led them to a corner table.

After they sat down, Paul ordered two glasses of wine. Gloria sipped the wine when it arrived but didn't lift the menu. He glanced up. "You know what you're going to have?"

She shook her head. "You decide for me." This evening was all about relaxing. She didn't even want to have to decide what to eat.

"Okay," he warned, "but don't blame me if you don't like it."

When the waiter returned, Paul ordered two of the dinner specials: tossed salad and baked lasagna with a side of garlic bread.

"Perfect," she assured him.

The conversation turned to the children, to the investigation, to the puppy mill and last, but not least, Dot's cancer.

Paul lifted his glass and sipped his wine. He eyed her over the rim of the glass. "You're worried."

Gloria sighed. "Very much." She couldn't imagine anything happening to her dear friend – to any of her friends. It seemed the worry had been sitting in the back of her mind, always there.

She knew that Pastor Nate had already talked to Dot and Ray and that he had added them to many prayer chains in the community and in the Town of Belhaven itself.

The meal arrived and it was delicious. The serving was twice what Gloria was accustomed to eating so they boxed the leftovers and headed to the truck.

Paul closed the door after Gloria slid into the passenger seat, walked around the truck and climbed into the driver's side. The air had a definite chill and Gloria pulled her jacket tighter as Paul turned the heat on "high."

"I'm thinking about buying a truck," she blurted out.

Paul shot her a sideways glance. That was the first time she had mentioned buying a truck. "You're going to get rid of Annabelle?"

She shook her head. Gloria would never part with Annabelle. She had already decided that if

– and when - Annabelle finally stopped running, she would store her in the barn. No, Annabelle would be around as long as Gloria still had breath in her lungs. "I'll never get rid of Annabelle but I was thinking that maybe I could get a truck to drive around in the winter. Something that's dependable."

Paul nodded. It was a good idea. "Okay. Let me know when you want to start looking and I'll go with you," he promised.

Paul pulled the truck into the drive and made his way to the passenger side. He glanced across the street as he opened the passenger door.

"Is someone moving in over there?" A light was on. The same light Gloria had noticed the night before.

Gloria grabbed his hand and slid out of the truck. "Something is going on. I've seen several cars over there but no moving truck." Of course, Gloria was gone a lot. Someone could have moved in and she just hadn't noticed.

Paul unlocked the kitchen door and opened it wide to let Mally out. She greeted them both and then raced across the yard to start her patrol.

Inside the house, Gloria stepped over to the kitchen counter. "Coffee?"

Paul shook his head. "I have to work in the morning."

Gloria's heart sank. What he meant was he had to work in a few hours. Morning to Paul was a shift that started at 4:00 a.m. "So you can't stay?"

"I'm afraid not." He reached over and pulled her close. "But don't worry. Soon enough you'll be stuck with me all the time and will be itching to get rid of me."

Gloria wrapped her arms around his neck. "I don't think so."

Paul leaned down and kissed her lips. It was a slow, tender, there's-so-much-more-to-come kiss that left Gloria breathless.

When he released his grip, she lifted a hand to her throat. "My goodness."

"There's more where that came from," he teased.

For once, Gloria was at a loss for words. She fiddled with the edge of her blouse as she followed him out onto the porch.

He gave her one final quick kiss and a warm hug before he turned and reluctantly made his way to the truck. It was getting harder and harder for Gloria to watch him go. Maybe because she knew soon, she wouldn't have to.

She waited until his taillights disappeared into the night before Mally and she headed back indoors.

Chapter 15

The drive to the Acosta's home in the country was about half an hour from Belhaven. Andrea had never technically worked on one of Gloria's investigations by herself. This one was important and Andrea was nervous that she might mess it up!

Alice could see Andrea was anxious. "We must make it sound good for Miss Gloria," Alice said.

Andrea tapped the steering wheel. "I know. The only problem is, I don't need another dog." Brutus was a handful. He was a good dog and Andrea loved him dearly but two dogs in the house, even a house as large as hers, was out of the question.

Alice adjusted her seatbelt. "No worries. We will figure it out."

Andrea pulled her shiny new pick-up truck into the drive and shut the engine off. She grabbed the door handle and turned to the woman who was like a second mother. She hoped they weren't walking into real danger. She would feel terrible if something went awry. "Ready for this?"

Alice nodded firmly. "Yes."

The women exited the pick-up truck and made their way across the weed-infested yard. Off in the distance, they could hear what sounded like a thousand barking dogs.

They made it as far as the edge of the yard when the side door opened and a tall man with a long black beard and piercing gray eyes met them at the top of the steps. "Can I help you?" The tone of his voice wasn't mean, but it was firm.

"I-I..." Andrea trailed off.

Alice stepped closer. "Yes, our friend told us she was here the other day and bought a puppy. We were wondering if you have any others for sale."

The man stepped off the porch. He narrowed his eyes and glanced at Andrea first. Then he turned to Alice. "You speak Spanish?" He had noticed her accent.

"Si," she replied.

The man smiled wide and began speaking in Spanish, talking 90 miles an hour. Andrea caught a word here or there. Words she had picked up over the years from Alice, but the conversation was flowing so fast that she couldn't keep up.

The man had relaxed his stance as he shoved his hands in his pockets and rocked back on his heels.

Andrea peeked at Alice out of the corner of her eye. Alice was enjoying the exchange. No one in the Town of Belhaven knew how to speak Spanish, as least as far as she knew.

Andrea caught the word "perro" a few times and knew that meant dog. Moments later, the man motioned them to follow him.

As they made their way along the side of the building and toward the back, the barks grew louder. Andrea wondered how many dogs were inside the place!

A combination lock secured the entrance door. The man twisted the dial back and forth and finally pulled down on the bottom. He unhooked the lock and pushed the door open.

Andrea took a deep breath and followed him inside. The first thing that struck her was the smell. A strong urine odor caught in her throat and she started to gag. She quickly clamped her hand over her mouth.

The man appeared not to notice.

Alice had a stronger stomach and the smell did not even faze her. She continued talking to the man in Spanish as they made their way down the long row of cages to the rear of the building.

The farther they walked, the darker the shed became...and the stronger the stench. There was zero air circulation in the back.

Andrea's heart sank at the sight of all of the poor creatures caged inside the building. Some of them pressed against the small cages, desperate for even an ounce of attention.

Others cowered in the back or curled up in a ball, barely moving at the sight of the three visitors.

Tears stung the back of Andrea's eyes. She closed them, willing the scene before her to disappear, but she knew in her heart what she was seeing would be with her for a very long time. No wonder Gloria had been distraught. This place was not fit for any living creature!

The man seemed proud of his animals as he wandered from cage-to-cage, pointing at various dogs and describing them in Spanish to Alice. She nodded several times. "Si."

When they finished their tour, the man stopped near the shed door. He pointed behind him.

"Usted quiere comprar un perro?"

Alice tilted her head towards Andrea. "He wants to know if we want to buy a dog."

"There are so many to choose from," Andrea said. "Can I talk it over with Alice and come back later?"

The man nodded. He said something else in Spanish and motioned them out of the building. He pulled the door closed and slid the lock through the slot. He snapped it shut and tugged on the bottom, making sure it was secure.

He held up a finger and headed back inside the house. "He's going to give us his telephone number," Alice explained.

He returned a moment later and handed a small slip of paper to Alice. After a few more exchanges, the women turned to go.

Safely inside the truck, and back on the road, Andrea spoke. "You have to tell me everything he said."

On the ride back to the house, Alice repeated the entire conversation.

***

The ringing of Gloria's phone awoke her the next morning. She leaned over and glanced at the clock beside her bed. It was already 8:30!

She flung back the covers, slipped her feet into her slippers and shuffled to the kitchen. By the time she got there, the phone had stopped ringing. It was Andrea and she could hear her voice as she left a message on the answering machine.

"Hi Gloria. I meant to call you last night. Alice and I went to the Acosta's farm yesterday and I wanted to report back."

Gloria grabbed her coffee tin from the back of the counter. She scooped a heaping spoonful into the top of the coffee maker, filled the carafe with water and dumped it into the back. She slid the carafe under the drip and turned it on.

While the coffee brewed, she picked up her house phone and dialed Andrea's cell phone.

"I hope I didn't wake you," Andrea fretted.

"It was time for me to get up," Gloria assured her.

She relayed the story of the visit to the puppy mill and that the owner spoke Spanish. "He took a liking to Alice and I think she enjoyed speaking to someone in her native tongue."

"The place was so sad, though," Andrea continued. "When I close my eyes, I can still see

200

those poor animals in the cages. It makes me want to bawl every time I think about it."

She went on. "Alice seems to think that he doesn't see anything wrong with the living conditions of those dogs. He is proud of his business. He believes that he is helping those poor animals, not hurting them."

How anyone could believe that the conditions of that puppy mill were acceptable was beyond Gloria's comprehension.

"She seems to think with a little guidance, that place could be turned into a thriving dog business...one that was good for the animals, not harmful."

Gloria could hear a second voice in the background.

"Hang on." Andrea covered the mouthpiece with her hand.

Moments later, she was back. "If you think about it, Alice does have a point. I mean, that huge old farm is a great place for dogs. Wouldn't it be something if they were able to turn it into some sort of training center, one that trained Seeing Eye dogs and companion dogs?"

Alice had taken the phone from Andrea. "Yes, Miss Gloria. The Acostas, they care for the animals but they have little money. I think with some guidance, they could turn that puppy mill into something good. Good for the dogs and the owners."

Gloria frowned. She had tossed around the idea of using some of her money for a worthy cause...something to help others. Perhaps the Lord was showing pointing her in the right direction.

Andrea had said several times that Alice rambled around the house and that she didn't have enough to keep her busy. What if, with a little of Gloria's money and Alice's help, they turned the Acosta's puppy mill into something completely different?

"I have an idea, Alice. Can you put the phone on speaker so that Andrea can hear?"

The girls spent several minutes brainstorming how Alice could approach the Acostas about turning the puppy mill into a thriving business – one that would help others AND the dogs. The more they talked, the more excited Gloria became.

She could invest some cash and Alice could invest her time. Before they hung up, Alice promised to do some on-line research on how to start a dog training service.

"I start now," Alice declared.

Andrea was back. "Hey..." There was a long pause.

"Oh my gosh! I've never seen Alice so excited," Andrea whispered into the phone. "She's already in the office starting her research."

Gloria was excited, too. Alice would not only help those poor animals, she would have purpose again AND help the disabled to boot! The whole project could be a win-win for everyone!

After she hung up the phone, she let Mally back in from her morning run.

She poured a cup of coffee and settled into the kitchen with her Bible. She turned to the concordance in the back and searched for the perfect verse:

"Do not be anxious about anything, but in every situation, by prayer and petition, with thanksgiving, present your requests to God." Philippians 4: 6-7 NIV

Gloria bowed her head and prayed for peace – and strength – for not only Dot but for herself, her family, her friends and for guidance with the dogs, which weighed heavy on her mind.

When she lifted her head, she felt better...better prepared to handle the upcoming days and weeks. She closed her Bible and slid it back onto the curio cabinet shelf.

Gloria shoved the kitchen chair across the floor and headed to the bathroom. It was time to start her day.

Chapter 16

By the time she finished showering and dressing, she had two more messages on her answering machine. One was from Jill and the other from Ruth. Both had asked her to call them back.

Gloria started with Jill, hoping that her daughter had followed through with her promise to call the real estate agent to let her know that they definitely wanted to move forward with the purchase of 726 Pine Place and to tell her they had scheduled an inspection for the following day.

Jill picked up on the first ring. "I did it! I told Sue Camp we were moving forward with the home purchase," she said triumphantly.

"Good!"

Jill went on. "Guess what? We *are* going to move forward with that house. Greg and I prayed about it together last night and feel that the Lord wants us to have that house!"

Praise the Lord! The God of all miracles was at work in the Rutherford household!

"I'm so glad, Jill. You were meant to have that house." Now, the neighbors, Gloria wasn't quite so sure about that. She remembered the big dog and the broken fence in the backyard...

"I called an inspection company and we're going to do the inspection day after tomorrow," Jill told her.

"Why not..."

"Because, if what you said was true - that someone is going to sabotage the house tonight thinking that we're going to have an inspection *tomorrow,* then we want to get in there before the inspector does, just to make sure things are ship shape."

Gloria grinned. She hadn't thought of that. Jill was right. "That's my girl," Gloria said proudly.

After she hung up the phone, she thanked the Lord for her kids...all of her kids. So far the day was shaping up to be perfect. Now if they could only get a good report on Dot's cancer...

Instead of calling Ruth back, Gloria decided that Mally and she would make a trip into town. She could kill two birds with one stone so-to-speak: check on Dot and stop by the post office to go over the plan for later that evening.

Gloria hadn't mentioned to Paul that they were setting up surveillance equipment in the house. She knew he would not approve of the plan and didn't want him to have to tell her not to do it when she knew that she would.

By the time Gloria made it into Belhaven, Dot's place was in between the breakfast and dinner rush. She pulled into the post office parking lot and wandered across the street.

Through the big picture window, she could see Dot as she darted back and forth behind the lattice that separated the back of the restaurant from the seating area.

The bell chimed when Gloria stepped inside and Dot paused, pot of coffee in hand. Gloria made her way to the back and waited while Dot set the coffee pot on the warmer. "How is Odie?"

Dot rolled her eyes. "Good heavens! That dog has taken over the Jenkins' household."

Gloria laughed. It sounded like her own house.

Dot placed her hands on her hips. "Can you believe that Ray lets that crazy dog sit at the kitchen table while we eat breakfast and even gives him his own plate?"

That did surprise Gloria a little. Ray was a neat freak. Everything had a place and he made sure that it stayed there. Of course, running your own business, one would almost have to be organized to some extent. Dot smoothed a stray strand of hair back in place. "They're in the back now."

Gloria shifted her purse to her shoulder. "When is the next doctor's appointment?" she asked.

The smile left Dot's face and Gloria was sorry she had mentioned it.

"We have an appointment Friday. They ran some more tests and the results will be back so the doctor wanted to go over them in person," Dot explained.

Gloria nodded. "I'll be praying."

She stopped in the kitchen to say hello to Ray and Odie before she gave Dot a quick hug and headed for the door.

Dot stopped her. "How is the investigation going?"

"Good," Gloria said. "Ruth is helping me with it later today."

Dot raised a brow. "Ruth. Don't tell me..." She waved a hand. "Nope. I don't want to know. I'm sure you have it all under control."

Gloria wasn't certain about that. She was a fly-by-the-seat-of-your-pants kind of sleuth. So far, it always seemed to work for her. One of these days, it would probably blow up in her face. She hoped that today wasn't one of them.

Gloria turned to go and then stopped. She lowered her voice. "Andrea and Alice visited the farm yesterday." She gave her a dark look.

"The farm? Oh! You mean the place out in the country." Dot caught on.

"Yep. Those two have a great plan. You won't believe what they came up with."

Dot shoved her hands in her apron pockets. "Hopefully something that will help those poor animals."

"Uh-huh." A couple entered the restaurant and settled into a booth near the front.

"I'll tell you later." Gloria headed out the door and across the street.

Ruth was inside, waiting on Sally Keane, one of the locals. The two leaned over the counter, their heads close together. Their conversation abruptly ended when Gloria stepped inside. Sally's eyes darted to Gloria. "I better go." The woman grabbed her purse and made a beeline for the door.

She looked guilty as all get out and from the look on Ruth's face; Gloria must have been the topic of conversation. She dropped her purse on the counter and turned to Ruth. There was no point in beating around the bush. "What was that all about?"

Ruth's eyes dropped. She rubbed an imaginary spot off the counter with her thumb. "Oh...nothing much."

"C'mon, Ruth. I know you better than that," Gloria cajoled.

Ruth sighed. "We were just talking about how lucky you girls were to come into that pile of money."

Gloria's brows formed a "V." Good ole Sally Keane was stirring the pot!

Ruth had seemed happy for the girls...all of them had. The last thing they needed was for someone – namely Sally Keane - to start making a fuss, jealous over something that Gloria, Margaret and Liz had no control over. They just happened to be in the right place at the right time.

Gloria frowned. "Let me guess. Sally thinks I should donate all the money to charity."

Ruth shrugged. "Something like that," she mumbled and lifted her gaze. "Listen. I think it's wonderful and you are not a selfish person by any means, Gloria, so whatever you do with that money is your business."

In Ruth's mind, the subject was closed. She grabbed a sheet of clean paper and set it on the counter. Next, she grabbed a pen from the holder and slid it forward. "I need a diagram of the house," she whispered, "so I can figure out the best place to put the you-know-what."

Gloria grabbed the piece of paper. "Why didn't I think of that?" She picked up the pen and began to sketch the layout of the house. When she finished, she slid it back across the counter.

Ruth slipped her reading glasses on and studied the paper. "Hmm." She looked up. "You're going to pick me up here at five?"

Gloria nodded. "On the dot." She turned to go. "Thanks for doing this for me. I know how much your spy equipment means to you."

Ruth shrugged. "You know I would do anything for you...for any of my friends."

Gloria smiled. "I know and I appreciate it." Without saying another word, Gloria slipped out of the post office and wandered back to her car.

She had one more stop: Margaret's place.

Chapter 17

Margaret's SUV was in the drive but when Gloria rang the bell, no one answered.

She made her way around the side of the garage and into the backyard. When she got to the back of the house, she found her friend settled into a patio chair with a cup of coffee and her Bible.

Gloria wandered onto the deck. "You read in the morning too."

Margaret slipped off her reading glasses. "Until the snow flies, I like to come out here in the morning." She gazed at the lake. "It's peaceful."

Mally made her way over to say "hi" and Margaret patted her head. "What brings you out this morning?" Gloria wasn't one to show up unannounced, but after running into Sally Keane in the post office this morning, something had stuck in Gloria's craw.

She settled into a chair across from Margaret while Mally darted toward the edge of the water to chase the ducks. "Have you heard any scuttlebutt about the money?"

Margaret closed her Bible, placed her hand on the top and sighed heavily. "You too?"

Gloria frowned. "Yeah. Apparently, Sally Keane is making her rounds, stirring up trouble. I caught her in the post office with Ruth. At first Ruth tried to deny it but she admitted that Sally had mentioned the money."

"Huh." Margaret didn't seem as concerned about the gossip as Gloria. Of course, Margaret's husband had retired a couple years back as vice president of a local bank and they already had money. Now they had more. "So you're feeling guilty."

"Somewhat," Gloria admitted.

"What do you propose we do?" Margaret asked.

"I have some ideas," Gloria said.

They talked for quite some time as they discussed how they could best help each of their friends. Gloria clapped her hands excitedly and jumped to her feet. "So we have a plan?"

The two of them had come up with good ideas: wonderful surprises for each of their friends. Now all Gloria needed to do was keep it secret long enough to put it all together!

Margaret walked Mally and Gloria to the car and waited while her friend climbed in the driver's seat. Gloria rolled down the window. "I'm thinking of buying a truck for the winter."

Margaret frowned. "You're going to get rid of Annabelle?"

Gloria shook her head. "Nope. I'll always have Annabelle but I was thinking a truck might be nice to get around in the winter on the snowy roads."

"You need one." Margaret had to agree. Out of all the friends, Gloria was the one that lived the farthest from town and there were days Gloria was stuck at home because the roads were impassable, at least for Annabelle.

Back in the day, Margaret used to worry about her friend driving on the treacherous roads but since cell phones came along, she didn't worry as much. If Gloria ended up in the ditch, she could call Gus, a Belhaven local, who owned a towing and automotive shop. Still, a truck would come in handy.

"You'll probably need it once you and Paul marry, what with moving furniture back and forth."

Gloria scratched her chin thoughtfully. *Would they* be moving furniture back and forth? So many details hadn't been settled yet.

Just take one day at a time, Gloria.

Back at the farm, Gloria rummaged around in the fridge for some lunchmeat and cheddar cheese. She grabbed two slices of bread from the package and stuck the rest in the refrigerator so it wouldn't go bad. Perhaps after Paul and she married, she would do a better job of stocking groceries. For the past several years, her diet consisted of sandwiches and frozen dinners. It made no sense to cook a big meal for just one person.

She placed the sandwich on a plate along with a small bag of chips and headed to the living room for the noon news. Now that the weather was starting to change, she liked to keep an eye on the forecast.

The weather looked clear and the news uneventful. Gloria finished her sandwich and carried the plate back to the kitchen. She was restless. She was always restless when it was detective day and today was an important one. Gloria's sanity was at stake!

She wondered if Ruth had finished mapping out the location of the spy equipment.

Gloria opened the dishwasher and placed the dirty plate on the bottom rack. She closed the door and turned to Mally. "Let's head to the barn."

It had been weeks since Gloria had been in her barn, not since her grandsons had come over for the weekend to work on their tree fort. Gloria turned her gaze to the front yard. She smiled at the color the boys had decided to paint the outside of the fort – florescent green.

Tyler and Ryan had come by the week before to finish the tree fort project. It was during that visit they decided to paint the exterior. She tried to talk them out of the bright green, but finally gave up. The three of them had gone to Nails and Knobs, the local hardware store, to purchase the paint the boys couldn't live without.

The bright color would fade through the long winter and by spring would turn into a nice shade of green that would hopefully blend in with the leaves on the tree.

Mally raced Gloria to the barn and stood outside the door, waiting for her to unlock the padlock and push the heavy door aside.

Gloria pulled it to the side, just enough to peek through the crack. Ever since the time she had discovered someone hiding out in her barn, she was leery to go in when she was at the farm all by herself.

The coast was clear and she tugged the door the rest of the way open. Mally went in first and began sniffing around. She trotted off to the milking parlor while Gloria stood in the doorway and surveyed the contents.

There was plenty of room inside. She'd had a garage sale not long ago and sold a bunch of stuff she no longer needed and that the kids didn't seem interested in inheriting.

She looked up at the old Massey Ferguson tractor and grinned as she remembered teaching Tyler and Ryan how to drive it.

Mally had finished her inspection and plopped down next to Gloria's feet. Mally had never been inside the tractor, let alone ridden in it.

Gloria bent down and patted her head, still staring at the bulky machinery. "You want to go for a spin?"

"Woof!"

The decision made, Gloria headed back to the house. She grabbed the tractor keys and her jacket, and Mally and she went back into the barn.

Gloria looked from Mally to the tractor. Her pooch had to weigh nearly fifty pounds! How on earth was she going to carry her dog up the steep steps to the cab of the tractor?

"Wait here." She climbed up the side and opened the door before she made her way back to the barn floor.

"This ought to be fun," she muttered. "Here goes nothing."

Gloria shoved the keys in her front pocket and lifted Mally. At first Mally wouldn't stop wiggling, which made it difficult for Gloria to hang onto her. "Settle down or no ride," she warned.

Mally immediately stopped moving and Gloria shifted her thick frame so that Mally's paws hung over her shoulder and Gloria had a firm grip on her backside.

Slowly, she made her way up the side steps. When she got to the top, she stopped. "Okay. Climb in."

Mally twisted at an angle then half hopped, half jumped into the cab, which sent Gloria reeling backward from the force of Mally's leap.

If not for the ironclad hold she had on the side handle, Gloria would have fallen off the tractor and tumbled backwards onto the concrete floor!

She nudged Mally to the side so they could share the seat and then pulled the door shut. "You better enjoy the ride because I don't think I can do this again," she warned, "not without breaking a few bones."

Gloria inserted the key in the ignition and turned it. The tractor fired on the first try.

She eased her foot off the clutch and pressed the gas. The tractor lurched forward and bumped off the curb.

They coasted around the drive a couple times. Mally seemed to have so much fun that Gloria decided to take the tractor for a spin out back.

She eased the clunky piece of farm equipment through the center of the empty fields, all the way to the edge of the property line.

They were on their final turn when something caught Gloria's eye. "Look, Mally! Deer!"

At the edge of the fence line, nibbling on withered stalks of corn were several deer, including a doe. Deer were a common sight around the farm and sometimes a nuisance when they went after Gloria's garden.

She kept deer repellant on hand and regularly sprayed the perimeter of the garden to keep them out. It worked like a charm and Gloria rarely had a problem with them eating her fruits and vegetables. It also kept the wild rabbits out, another pesky critter that loved the goodies in Gloria's garden.

The deer were brave to be out right now. Bow season had just ended and gun season would start up in a couple weeks.

Mally leaned across the armrest, pressed her nose to the window and kept a close eye on the animals until they were out of sight.

Gloria backed the tractor into the barn, shut off the engine and opened the door. Getting Mally out of the tractor was going to be as tricky as getting her in.

Her eyes scanned the interior of the barn and stopped when she found something that might work to get Mally out without Gloria having to carry her.

Several years ago when they had chickens and a chicken coop, James had built an old ramp. "Wait here."

Gloria scrambled out of the tractor. She dragged the ramp over to the tractor, leaned one end of the ramp against the door and placed the other end on the cement floor. "Can you come down?"

Mally looked at the ramp, placed one paw on the ramp and then pulled it back.

Gloria lifted her end of ramp until it was level with the other end, which rested on the floor of the cab. "C'mon girl," she coaxed.

Mally put one paw, then another on the ramp as she tentatively crept along the wooden walkway. The closer she got to Gloria, the lower Gloria moved the ramp. By the time Mally got to the end, it was resting on the cement floor. They had done it!

"Good girl!"

"Ruff." Mally licked her hand and pranced around.

Gloria crawled back inside the tractor, pulled the keys from the ignition and closed the door. She waited until Mally was out of the barn before securing the barn door and snapping the padlock in place.

Gloria was halfway to the house when something across the street caught her attention. There were cars in the drive and she could see someone standing next to one of the vehicles. "Shall we go meet the new neighbors?"

She didn't wait for a reply and the two of them headed across the road.

Chapter 18

Parked in the drive was a new sedan. Standing next to the car was a young couple. They turned as Gloria approached. "Hello, I'm Gloria Rutherford. I live across the street."

The woman smiled, her long dark hair falling forward, covering a bright blue eye. She shifted the baby she was holding in her arms. "Hello. I'm Melody Fowler and this is my husband, Chris."

Gloria smiled at them as she patted Mally's head. "This is Mally."

The woman reached her hand forward so Mally could sniff. Mally licked her palm...the Mally seal of approval.

The man stuck his hand out and Mally did the same. "Hello Mally. What a beautiful dog."

Gloria knew her dog was a good judge of character so if Mally liked them, she was sure she would. "Are you moving in?"

The man, Chris, shook his head. "Not yet. We're doing some renovations first."

Gloria glanced at the house. "This farm once belonged to my husband's family. He sold it to one of the local farmers years ago, but I don't believe anyone ever moved into the house."

"It needs updating," the young woman admitted.

They exchanged a few pleasantries and Gloria turned to go. "I better get going. I'm sure you have work to do. Let me know if I can help," she called out as she wandered back across the street.

It would be nice to have neighbors again. They seemed like a friendly couple and the baby was cuter than a button.

She had wondered what kind of renovations they planned but didn't want to seem nosy. It had been years since Gloria had been inside the house.

She couldn't date the house but knew it was at least a hundred years old and a lot of the house was original: the plumbing, electrical, mechanicals, not to mention old wallpaper, paneling and carpet.

Now that she thought about it, it could probably use a major overhaul. She hoped they got a good deal!

The rest of the afternoon crawled by. When 4:30 rolled around, Gloria changed into dark slacks and a navy blue sweater – the perfect attire for an undercover operation. Although this wasn't an undercover operation, it was a habit to wear dark clothes. Sleuthing and dark clothing just seemed to go together.

Gloria steered Annabelle to the back of the post office parking lot and pulled in next to Ruth's car to wait.

At 5:01, Ruth exited the rear of the post office carrying a large cardboard box. She opened the rear passenger door and slid the box onto the seat before she climbed into the passenger side. She pulled the seatbelt across her lap and fastened the buckle. "I'm nervous as a tic."

Gloria grinned and started the car. "If you're nervous now, just wait."

On the drive to Rapid Creek, Ruth outlined her strategy. She patted her pocket. "I have the drawing with me...just in case. I was able to do a little research online and found a rough blueprint for this house. It was built by a local company."

Gloria snorted. "You're kidding."

"No." Ruth's expression grew serious. "Mechanicals are very important when installing surveillance equipment."

Gloria hadn't considered that. "Will you need electricity?" She couldn't remember if the power had been shut off.

Ruth shook her head. "Nope. The surveillance equipment runs on electricity and has a battery backup but it will only last a day or so."

Gloria turned Annabelle onto the main road and pressed down on the gas pedal. "We're going to pick the equipment up tomorrow so that shouldn't be a problem."

Gloria had already given some thought as to how they should enter the house. They could pull in the driveway but if the neighbors spotted them...

She was torn. On one hand, she could come up with an excuse for being there. On the other, she didn't want the suspect - or suspects - to see them enter the house, carrying a large box. She erred on the side of caution and decided to park one street over, directly behind the property.

They pulled onto the side street and climbed out of the car. Ruth reached into the back of the car and pulled out her box of surveillance equipment.

Gloria frowned. She wished she had thought to bring a backpack or something that was less conspicuous. Lucy would have definitely thought of that!

It was too late now. "This way." She waved Ruth to follow as they walked between two houses and made their way to the back yard.

A rickety fence ran along both sides of the property but the back perimeter was wide open. They stepped into the backyard and something squished under Gloria's sneaker. She lifted her foot to inspect the bottom of her shoe. Whatever it was, was dark brown and mushy.

"I think I just stepped on a landmine," she groaned.

Ruth leaned forward for a closer look. "Yep. That is definitely dog doo."

She began to gag when she got a good whiff of the brown squishy stuff on Gloria's shoe. "Oh no!" Ruth covered her mouth and turned away, all the while still making the gagging noises.

"Shush! You're going to blow our cover," Gloria whispered fiercely as she scraped her foot along the grass to remove as much of the poo as possible.

Ruth sucked in a breath of fresh air. "I'm sorry. I've always had an overactive gag reflex."

"Don't ever get a pet," Gloria warned.

"Let's get this over with." She motioned Ruth along and the women tiptoed through the rest of the yard as they made their way to the rear slider.

Gloria tugged on the handle. The door was locked.

She remembered that the basement door had been unlocked last time she was there. Then she remembered that Jill and she had locked it before they left.

Still, it was worth a try. "Wait here," she told Ruth.

She wandered to the side window and stuck her finger on the ledge. It didn't budge.

Gloria's heart sank. That meant she would have to go to the front of the house and enter through the front door.

Gloria closed her eyes and whispered a quick prayer that she would make it inside undetected.

She walked around the side of the house and picked up the pace as she headed to the front porch. She twisted the knob on the combination lock and then yanked on the base.

The key dropped into her hand. She inserted the key, opened the door and stepped inside. Safely inside, she peeked out the front window. No one was in sight.

Ruth peered at Gloria through the rear slider. She waited while her friend scooted across the dining room floor, flipped the lever lock and slid the door open.

Ruth stepped inside and looked around. "Just as I envisioned." She set the box on the kitchen counter and began pulling equipment from the box and placing it on the counter.

"What can I do to help?" Gloria reached for the box. The sooner they could get the spy gear set up, the sooner they could get out of there.

Ruth shook her head. "Nothing. It would take too long to explain."

Gloria pulled her hand back. "Okay. No problem."

While Ruth worked on the installation, Gloria headed to the front door and replaced the key in the container then put the lockbox back on the door. She closed the front door and tugged on the handle to make sure it had locked.

She stood off to one side and watched Ruth work, impressed by her speed and efficiency. Ruth had it down to a science!

Ruth had almost finished her installation when Gloria had a thought. Perhaps she should unlock the basement window again to give the would-be perpetrator a way to get in.

"Almost done," Ruth announced.

"I'll be right back." Gloria hustled down the basement steps and to the bedroom in the back. She unlatched the window and headed back up the stairs.

Ruth was waiting at the top, the empty box tucked under her arm. "Mission accomplished."

Gloria didn't want to leave using the front door, not with Ruth holding a large brown box. She opened the rear slider. "Wait for me out here."

Ruth stepped onto the back deck.

Gloria pulled the door shut and locked the door behind her. If her goal was to avoid detection, there was only one way out.

Gloria headed back down the basement steps to the window she had just unlocked. She lifted the window and grimaced. "Here goes nothing."

She hoisted herself up onto the window frame, her legs dangling in the air behind her as she desperately tried to pull her body through the opening.

A rustling on the other side of the fence caught her attention.

Gloria tipped her head to peer through a small gap between two of the boards. Her eyes widened in horror. There, on the other side of the fence was a large black eye and sharp canine teeth.

"Grr!"

Chapter 19

Gloria put a finger to her lips. "Shhh, puppy. I'm almost out of here," her raspy voice giving way to her fear. Trying to soothe the dog seemed to have the opposite effect and make him even more agitated. The mutt began to bark his fool head off.

"*Woof! Woof-Woof!*"

Gloria dragged one knee onto the frame and pulled herself across the metal barrier.

The dog, focused on Gloria's every move, began to ram his head against the wooden panel as he tried to get to Gloria.

"What in the world are you doing?"

Shiny black shoes stepped into Gloria's range of vision. Her eyes traveled from the shoes and up the pant legs to the top of a uniform...a police uniform. A very *familiar* police uniform.

Paul knelt on the ground. He blew a puff of air through thinned lips. "I would offer to help but it looks like you have it all under control."

Paul stood upright, grabbed his radio and unclipped it from his belt. "Yes, this is Officer Kennedy. Disregard the 10-14."

He clipped the radio to his belt and grimaced as his fiancé rose to her feet and brushed the dirt from her dark slacks. "A neighbor reported a suspicious person prowling around the house."

The dog, still on the other side of the fence, began to growl. Paul glanced across the fence. "Let's move to the back so the dog will stop barking."

Gloria nodded. She lowered the window frame and followed him to the back yard where Ruth was waiting on the rear deck.

"This just keeps getting better and better," Paul muttered under his breath.

He tipped his hat to Ruth. "Hello Ruth."

Ruth shifted the box in her hands. "Hello Paul. Nice to see you."

Gloria gave her a hard stare.

Ruth swallowed hard and lowered her gaze. "Or maybe not."

He turned his attention to Gloria. "Do you want to explain to me why you were sneaking out of this house and why Ruth is carrying an empty box, looking guiltier than a fox in a hen house?"

"Well..."

Paul lifted a hand. "Let me guess." He waved his hand towards the house. "This is the house that Jill intends to buy."

Gloria nodded. It was best not to say too much. She knew he had caught her red-handed. Hopefully he wouldn't force them remove the spy equipment...

He pointed to the box Ruth was holding. "I don't even want to know what that is for."

Gloria let out a sigh of relief. "It's probably best."

He jerked his head to the house next door, the one with the barking dog. "The neighbor next door appears to be keeping an eye on this place," he warned.

"Thanks for the tip," Ruth piped up.

Gloria gave her a warning look. She turned to Paul. "We'll be on our way now."

Paul followed the women through the backyard and over to Gloria's car. He waited for Gloria to slide into the driver's seat and roll down the window. "Please don't make me come back here again," he said.

Gloria nodded. She couldn't promise him anything. After all, they had to come back tomorrow to retrieve Ruth's equipment. "We'll do our best." She smiled brightly.

Paul rolled his eyes. "That's what I was afraid you would say."

The girls pulled out of the neighborhood and Gloria followed Paul's police car out onto the main road. "That went off fairly well," Ruth observed.

Despite the minor snag of running into Paul, Gloria had to agree. "Yes. As well as can be expected."

On her way out of the neighborhood, they passed a familiar car. Gloria glanced in her rearview mirror. "That car looks just like the one Sue Camp, Jill's real estate agent, drives."

The car turned onto Pine Place and disappeared from sight.

Annabelle drifted toward the center of the road. "Watch where you're going," Ruth yelled.

Gloria yanked the car back into her lane. "Sorry about that!"

On the drive back to Belhaven, Ruth explained that the equipment was motion activated so she wouldn't have to watch the screen constantly, like she had done when she set up the surveillance equipment at Gloria's house a few months back. "It gives off a warning beep to let me know the camera picked up movement."

Gloria frowned. "You leave it on all the time – day and night?"

Ruth set her purse on the floor. "Yeah. I'm used to it, though. I leave it on at the post office all night."

"Doesn't it have a recorder? What if it goes off while you're sleeping?"

"I like to catch the action live. It's loud enough to wake me." Ruth shrugged. "I just get up and check the monitor then go back to bed."

Gloria glanced at her friend out of the corner of her eye. She knew Ruth was obsessed with her surveillance equipment but this was taking it to the extreme!

Gloria pulled her car next to Ruth's van and waited while her friend pulled the empty box from the backseat. "A backpack might work better. You know, so it's not quite so obvious," Gloria hinted.

Ruth nodded. "Yeah, you're right. I never thought of that…"

Ruth closed the back door and leaned her head in the front window. "I'll text you if I catch anything on the camera."

She pulled the van door open, tossed the box in the passenger seat and climbed in the driver's seat. She gave Gloria a small wave and backed out of her parking spot.

Gloria waited until the van had turned onto Main Street before she pulled out onto the road and headed home, all the while praying that they would finally get a break in the case!

Chapter 20

Gloria waited for Paul's evening phone call with a hint of dread. She wondered if he would mention the incident from earlier and was relieved when he didn't. The only thing he said was he hoped for her sake that Jill got the house.

She kept her cell phone close by in the hopes that Ruth's surveillance equipment would do the trick and they would catch someone breaking into the house.

She stayed up until after the 11:00 news. Ruth never called. Gloria finally gave up and fell asleep in the recliner. The cuckoo clock chimed midnight and Gloria woke.

Mally was sprawled across Gloria's lap. She opened one eye and stared a Gloria.

Gloria shifted her legs. "C'mon, girl. It's time for bed."

Mally eased out of the recliner, straightened her paws out in front of her and stretched her long limbs.

By the time Gloria brushed her teeth and washed her face, Puddles had already curled up in her favorite spot on the pillow and Mally was asleep at the end of the bed.

Gloria sandwiched herself between her two pets and promptly drifted off to sleep.

***

Chirp...chirp...chirp.

Bright sunlight streamed through the bedroom window. Gloria had forgotten to close the curtains before she crawled into bed. She groggily glanced at the clock on the nightstand. It was 6:30 a.m.

Chirp.

Gloria flung the covers aside when she realized it was her cell phone! She shuffled over to the

249

dresser and picked up the phone. There were several text messages. Gloria carried the phone to the kitchen, slipped on her reading glasses and stared at the screen.

All of the messages were from Ruth. The first one read: "I just saw something." The time stamp was 2:48 a.m.

She scrolled to the second message. "You are not gonna believe what just happened!" That message arrived at 3:12 a.m.

Ruth sent the third and final message at 3:22 a.m. "Stop by the post office ASAP in the morning!"

The post office opened at 8:00 a.m., although she knew that Ruth was at work earlier than 8:00 a.m. Kenny Webber, the rural route carrier, and she arrived early to sort mail and get ready for the day.

She threw on the first thing she found in her closet, grabbed her keys and headed out the door.

It was mornings like that she wished the small town had a fast food restaurant with a drive-thru or even a coffee shop.

It was 7:22 a.m. according to Gloria's dashboard when she pulled in the post office parking lot. Dot's place was already busy with early morning diners. Many of the local farmers showed up as soon as she unlocked the doors, having already milked the cows and tended to their livestock.

She wandered around the back and tapped on the employee entrance. Kenny opened the door a crack. He smiled when he saw Gloria. "Ruth said you were stopping by." He swung the door open and Gloria stepped inside.

Ruth, her back to Gloria, shoved an envelope into one of the mailboxes and then set the rest of the stack on the sorting table. She waved Gloria to the small desk in the back. "Wait 'til you see this!"

Gloria gave Kenny a quick glance.

"Kenny knows all about the surveillance. He noticed my equipment was missing this morning."

Gloria grinned. Kenny was a good guy and Ruth's right hand man. She was sure that Kenny had many stories he could tell about the goings on inside that little post office! He probably knew more about Gloria than she knew about herself!

She stepped over to the computer screen and slipped on her reading glasses. The screen was dark. Gloria watched closely, waiting for something to happen. *Was she missing something?* "What am I looking at?"

"Just wait," Ruth replied.

Seconds later, a small light beamed onto the screen. Gloria could tell from the angle that it was coming up the basement steps. The beam flashed around the room like a light show on steroids before it settled on the kitchen.

The intruder set the flashlight on the counter so that the light illuminated the ceiling. There were several long moments of silence followed by several loud whacks.

"What in the world…"

It was hard to see through the dark grainy computer screen, but the sound was loud and clear. After what seemed like an eternity, the whacking stopped.

The person picked up the flashlight and turned the light to the kitchen cabinets. Gloria realized with horror what the whacking noise was. The intruder had smashed some of the fronts on the lower kitchen cabinets while others appeared to be completely missing! Splintered chunks of wood scattered the floor. "Oh no!"

Her heart plummeted. What would possess someone to destroy a home like that?

"Can we watch it again?" she asked.

Ruth glanced at the clock. It was 7:50 a.m. "Yeah, I have a few minutes before I have to unlock the front doors."

She fiddled with the mouse and set the surveillance video back to the beginning. Gloria leaned forward, searching for a clue...anything that might help them figure out who this person might be.

She couldn't come up with anything. She waited until the flashlight and dark figure disappeared down the stairs before she turned to Ruth. "Was that it?"

Ruth nodded. "Yep."

Gloria stood upright and gazed out the front window. "We have two problems now," she said.

Ruth lowered the laptop cover. "What's that?"

Gloria lifted a finger. "One, we don't know who that was." She lifted a second finger. "Two, as far as anyone knows, we were the last two people inside that house!"

There was the possibility they could be charged with destruction of property, theft, breaking and entering, unlawful use of surveillance equipment...although she wasn't certain of that.

Ruth shook her head. "No. We are down to just one problem. There was a big clue and I'm surprised that you missed it."

Chapter 21

Gloria frowned. "What clue?"

Ruth let out a dramatic sigh and lifted the top of the computer. "Gloria, Gloria, Gloria, are you losing your touch?" she teased.

"I'll cover the front," Kenny offered.

Ruth acknowledged him briefly. "Thanks, Kenny."

She turned back to the screen and started the video from the beginning.

The light bounced up the stairs and started across the room.

"Close your eyes and just listen," Ruth urged.

Gloria closed her eyes and focused on the sounds. This time, she heard it: a faint scraping sound, as if the person was dragging something across the tile floor. "Yeah, I hear it."

Ruth crossed her arms. "Whoever was in that house either dragged the sledgehammer OR what I think, is that they walked with a limp."

"Hmm." It was a stretch.

Ruth fast-forwarded to the end. "You can hear it again."

Sure enough, towards the end of the video, they heard the distinct sound of something dragging.

It was a good clue, but how in the world could they figure out who it was? It could be anyone. For all they knew, the person could have driven their car from the other side of the state and snuck in, just like Gloria and Ruth had done.

The fact that the intruder had destroyed the kitchen cabinets and stolen the rest was scary. Leaving a dead animal or two was bad enough...

Ding. A customer had walked into the post office. "Be right back."

Ruth headed to the counter to help the customer while Gloria stared out the window. All she could visualize was Jill, Greg, Ryan, Tyler, Eddie, Karen, Ben, Kelly, Oliver and Ariel, along with Gloria and Paul all trying to cram into her house.

Ruth returned. "I think it's one of the neighbors."

She had Gloria's undivided attention and pressed on. "Think about it. Who else could it be? I doubt it's the homeowners, especially now that whoever it was destroyed the kitchen cabinets. It's one thing to try to drive away buyers so you can keep collecting the deposit, but it's a completely different story when they start destroying stuff. I mean, those homeowners will have to pay to have the cabinets repaired and the missing ones replaced."

True. Ruth had a valid point. It would be completely counterproductive. On top of that, Gloria had seen the house the Acostas lived in. If they were collecting deposits for cash flow, they weren't using the money to improve their current living conditions.

"Plus, whoever it is knows the comings and goings of that place, which would point right to a neighbor, someone who can watch the place."

Gloria thought about the neighbors she had met. On one side, the people had seemed quite friendly and informative. Gloria didn't get the impression that they had hard feelings towards the Acostas. In fact, it seemed quite the opposite.

There was the nice woman on one side of course, she was the one that had called the police on Ruth and her.

Then there was the older couple across the street, the ones who had pets of their own.

Last, but not least, there were the noisy neighbors on the other side. The ones with the big dogs and the flimsy fence that separated their property from the one Jill and Greg intended to buy. She had never met the people who lived in that house, only the boy who had come to the door.

"So we're looking for someone with a limp. What do you suggest that we do? Go door-to-door asking the neighbors if they walk with a limp?"

Ruth shook her head. "Nope. I've been giving this some thought." She held out her hand. "Be right back."

Gloria watched her disappear in the back room. Kenny watched her go. "Wait 'til you see this," he said.

Gloria could hardly wait.

Ruth returned with a large, shiny, plastic copter. "This is a DR650, able to fly up to 250 feet. It has a 720 x 240 resolution that can take 3MP photos and video tape for a full five minutes."

Gloria stared at the contraption in confusion.

Kenny touched one of the propellers with his index finger and gave it a spin. "It's a drone."

"A drone?" Gloria had seen drones on the local news in recent weeks. They were a nuisance for airplanes at the Grand Rapids Airport. Pilots had reported several near misses with drones when they accidentally wandered into the planes' flight paths.

From what little she knew, Gloria considered them a dangerous toy. She could tell from the look on Ruth's face that Ruth did not consider her drone to be a toy!

Ruth carefully placed the drone on the counter. "We can use this to film aerial footage of the neighbors. They won't even know it's there."

Gloria stared at the drone. An idea began to form in her head. "So we come up with some kind of lure to draw the neighbors out of their houses. The drone is overhead, capturing their

261

movements on camera. Whoever shows up on video with a visible limp..."

Ruth snapped her fingers. "Voila! We have our man. Or woman." she added.

The bell chimed again. Gloria waited while Ruth took care of the customers. She nodded to Judith Arnett, who was one of them.

When Sally Keane walked in, Gloria glared at her then turned her back. She was the last person Gloria wanted to see!

Sally made a quick exit after checking her mailbox.

Kenny had finished sorting his mail, organizing it in the large plastic bins and then loading the bins into his mail truck. He came back to grab his keys.

Gloria stepped to the side, out of view of the lobby.

Kenny walked over and whispered in Gloria's ear. "I've got a few 4th of July fireworks left over if you want to use them." He winked and then turned on his heel, whistling a catchy tune as he exited the post office and climbed into the mail truck.

Ruth caught the tail end of the conversation. "We might want to take him up on that."

Gloria slowly nodded. They would need something to draw the suspects out into the open. She turned to Ruth. "Can you forward a copy of that videotape to me?"

"Of course." Ruth settled into the desk chair. She clicked a few buttons and turned to Gloria. "Done. I emailed a copy to you."

"Thanks." Gloria reached for the door handle. "When do you want to pick up the spy equipment?"

She remembered Jill telling her that she had scheduled an inspection of the house for the following day. "Maybe we can run by there before Jill's inspection. How long do you think it will take?"

Ruth stared at the ceiling. "I'm guessing no more than 20 minutes. Tops."

Gloria stared at the back door thoughtfully. They could pick up the spy equipment and implement their plan to flush out the perpetrator at the same time.

She opened the door. "Yeah. We can do it tomorrow morning." That would be perfect. "Ask Kenny to drop off the fireworks, just in case."

Ruth nodded. "Got it covered. Want to swing by my house say around 10?"

Gloria pulled her keys from her purse. "Yeah, that'll work. I'll see you in the morning."

Gloria climbed into her car and started the engine. Her next stop was Montbay County Sheriff's office to visit Paul.

Gloria settled into the chair across from her betrothed. He leaned his elbows on the desk and clasped his hands in front of him. Gloria wasn't one to drop by for a casual social visit, not while he was at work. He was certain the reason she was there had something to do with Jill and the house.

Paul got right to the point. "Something happened," he stated bluntly.

Gloria rubbed the palms of her hands on the front of her slacks. "Yeah. The box that Ruth had yesterday... You got a minute for me to show you something on the computer?"

Paul nodded. "Sure."

Gloria inched her way around the desk and leaned over Paul's keyboard. "Do you mind if I log into my email account?"

"Be my guest."

Gloria opened her email and scrolled through the messages until she got to the one Ruth had sent her. She opened the message and clicked on the attachment. "Watch this."

Gloria pressed the "play" button and stepped back.

Paul leaned forward. He watched the video in silence and then pressed the stop button. "This is what you and Ruth were doing yesterday? Installing surveillance equipment?"

Gloria cringed inwardly and nodded. "Did you notice anything about the person?"

Paul played the video again. "Whoever it was walked with a limp."

"Right. Do you think you can question the neighbors?" Gloria would love to hand it over to Paul. It wasn't that she didn't want to be involved, but the fact that they had been inside the house right before it had been broken into and vandalized would make Ruth and her prime suspects.

Paul forwarded the video to his own email then clicked out of hers. He shook his head. "Unfortunately, our hands are tied, unless, of course, the homeowners file a report."

She frowned. Maybe they would. Maybe they wouldn't, although if they were to file an insurance claim, they would have to file a police report. She wasn't sure how long that would take. It could take weeks! Gloria didn't have weeks - she had hours!

Her shoulders drooped. "It was worth a try."

Paul knew Gloria was not going to let this go. "What are you going to do now?"

"We think it's a neighbor." She shrugged. "We only have one choice...flush the perpetrator out."

"How do you propose to do that?" He paused. "Never mind. I don't think I want to know."

Paul got out of his chair and followed Gloria down the hall and out to the main lobby. "Please be careful. When do you plan to 'flush them out?'" If he knew "when," at least he could be on the alert in case she needed help.

"Tomorrow morning, right after we pick up the surveillance equipment."

Paul gave Gloria a quick kiss and held the door. He shook his head and slowly closed the door behind her. She sure did know how to keep him on his toes.

Chapter 22

Gloria made a pit stop at Lucy's on her way home. Lucy, the closest to an explosives expert that Gloria could come up with, might have an idea on how to attract attention without blowing – say – a hand or other body part - off in the process.

She parked Annabelle behind Lucy's jeep and started down the sidewalk.

Brrrup!

Gloria stopped in her tracks.

Brrrup!

That noise. It was coming from the direction of the shed.

She could see that the shed door was open.

Brrrup!

It had to be Lucy.

Gloria wandered around the corner and spotted her friend, bent over her workbench. Lucy was wearing a metal welding mask. Gloria burst out laughing at the sight of the mask. Protruding out of both sides of the mask were two deer antlers – one on each side.

Lucy dropped the welding gun and jumped back. "You scared the crap out of me!"

She lifted the mask and clutched her chest. "I almost had a heart attack!"

Gloria patted her arm. "I'm sorry, Lucy," she apologized. She pointed at the antlers. "Don't tell me those are from a deer that you shot."

Lucy ran her hand along one of the antlers. "Yep," she said proudly. "A four point buck."

"Are you going hunting this year?"

Gun season ran from mid-November until the end of November. Last year, Lucy had gone hunting with her ex-boyfriend, Bill. They had broken up not long ago, right after Lucy told him she didn't want to go bow hunting, but instead wanted to hang out with the girls.

Bill had never been one of Gloria's favorite people and she always thought that Lucy always went along with whatever Bill wanted but he would never do anything that she wanted to do. It was a one-sided relationship, not that she had ever admitted that to her friend.

Lucy wrinkled her nose. "I'm not sure. I don't want to go alone and Max doesn't sound too enthused about it."

Her eyes sparked. "Hey! Why don't you go with me?"

Gloria shook her head. "Oh no! I don't…"

Lucy clasped her hands together. "Please," she begged. "You need more shooting practice and I need someone to go with me. It'll be fun."

Gloria sucked in a deep breath. Lucy had always been a good sport about helping Gloria out with her investigations and had asked for little in return. In fact, this was the first time Gloria could remember her ever asking for a favor...

"Well, maybe," she conceded.

Lucy bounced on her toes. "Oh, thank you, Gloria! It's going to be so much fun," she gushed.

Gloria slowly shook her head, certain she would rue the day this day. Deep down, Gloria knew she would go if it meant that much to her friend.

She pointed at pieces of metal sitting on top of the workbench. "Whatcha building?"

Lucy lifted two bars she had just welded together. "Wait 'til you see what I'm making."

She stepped over to the wall and dragged two pieces of barn wood to the center of the floor. "It's going to be a small table. I'm going to put it out on the porch. Since this is my first welding project, I thought I'd start small," Lucy explained.

Gloria wrinkled her nose. A table didn't sound small. Wall art or jewelry holder - that was small.

"When I'm done with this, I want to build a fire pit out of old tire rims. I found a picture of one on the internet and I've already got the rims."

"Sounds cool, Lucy. I can't wait to see it," Gloria said.

"Yeah, I kinda need a hobby. I was thinking I could start making some stuff and selling it at the flea market during the summer months."

"Do you need some money?" Gloria had never heard her friend mention money being tight and Gloria had never asked.

"Nah." Lucy shrugged. "I need something to keep me busy during the winter." She pointed to a cast iron wood stove in the corner. "I can come out here and work when it's nasty outside."

Jasper tromped into the garage, his paws covered in a thick coat of fresh mud.

Lucy stuck her hand on her hip. "Jasper! What did you get into this time?"

Jasper hung his head and looked up at Lucy guiltily.

Gloria reached over and patted his head. "There's so much fun stuff to get into living out here in the country, huh?"

She looked up at Lucy. "Don't worry. The newness will wear off and he'll settle down. Just tell him no and soon he'll understand what he can and can't get into. Labs are smart dogs."

Jasper slumped into a heap at Lucy's feet and let out a sigh. "He sure does wear himself out."

She changed the subject. "So what brings you by?"

The women stepped out of the garage. Lucy shut off the lights and closed the door, locking it behind her. Jasper led the way as the three of them headed to the house.

Inside the kitchen, Lucy pulled a plate from the microwave and set it on the table. "Monster cookie? I made them this morning."

Gloria plucked a candy-coated cookie from the plate and took a bite. "I love cookies with nuts. These are delicious. What's in them?"

Lucy pulled a large cookie from the plate and nibbled the edge. "My grandmother's secret recipe," she said.

Gloria wasn't nearly as fond of sweets as Lucy, but these were delicious. She reached for another one.

Lucy grinned. "Wow! You must like them."

"Either that or I'm starving." She eyed the cookie before breaking a chunk off and popping it into her mouth.

Lucy reached for another cookie. "So what's going on?"

Lucy listened while Gloria explained everything that had happened. She started with the surveillance equipment Ruth had installed yesterday and ended with her visit to the police station and how there was nothing Paul could do until the homeowner filed a report.

"So you're going to take matters into your own hands to try and flush out the perpetrator," Lucy surmised.

"Exactly and since you're an explosives expert, I thought I would get your professional opinion," Gloria said.

Lucy drummed her fingers on the tabletop thoughtfully. "The plan is to have the drone circle over the top of the neighbors' houses and then set off some kind of bait to lure them out."

She gazed out the window. "The only problem is, once you ignite one set of explosives, how are you going to sneak into the neighbor's yard across the street and do the same thing? I mean, it will be loud and everyone is going to hear it."

Gloria rubbed her temple. True. She hadn't thought of that. Maybe they could set the explosive off in the middle of the street and all of the neighbors would come running out to see what was going on.

"What about putting a trash can in the middle of the street and blowing it up?" Gloria was thinking aloud.

"Nope. Someone might see you and then you risk getting arrested."

The dilemma had Lucy and Gloria stumped. Gloria needed a plan and she needed it by morning. "Maybe I'll go home and sleep on it," she said.

Lucy and Jasper walked Gloria to her car. "If I come up with an idea, I'll let you know," Lucy promised as she waited for Gloria to climb in the car.

Lucy brightened. "You want me to go with you?"

Gloria started the car and rolled the window down before she shut the door. Lucy looked so excited; Gloria didn't have the heart to tell her no. "Sure. The more the merrier."

"I'll pick you up around ten," she added.

"Great." Lucy gave a small wave and then headed back inside.

Gloria pulled out of the drive and onto the road. *Please, God. Help us come up with some sort of idea on how to flush out the culprit.*

She turned into her drive and pulled into the garage. Maybe if she watched a couple episodes of *Detective on the Side,* she might come up with an idea or two.

Chapter 23

Gloria finally came up with a plan but she didn't get it from her favorite detective show. She got her brilliant idea while she was on the back porch waiting for Mally to fetch the newspaper from the drive. It was when a school bus drove by the house.

Gloria took the paper from Mally and exchanged it for a doggie treat.

When they got indoors, she promptly called the local high school to ask what time the bus dropped students off at the Highland Park subdivision. After she had that information, she called the girls to change the pick-up time to 2:45 p.m. They would arrive at Highland Park just in time for the bus to drop the neighborhood students off.

Ruth's work schedule ended at five but Kenny said he could make it back in time to cover for her.

Ruth was the designated driver, and the women arrived at the neighborhood a little ahead of schedule. She pulled her van to the end of the street and parked near the entrance.

The women waited patiently for the familiar bright yellow and black striped bus.

When it rounded the corner and stopped at the end of the cul-de-sac, Gloria unhooked her seatbelt and reached for the door handle. "Wait here." She didn't want to raise suspicion by having them all get out and on top of that, she wasn't even certain who she was looking for.

She stepped around the front of the van and waited on the sidewalk as high schoolers exited the bus and began to wander down the sidewalk.

A young blonde wearing ear buds and staring at the ground stepped off. Gloria studied her briefly and scratched her from the list. *She wasn't at all observant.*

Next were a boy and girl, who started to quarrel as soon as they hit the pavement. *Brother and sister, plus I don't have enough cash.* Scratch #2.

A teenager darted off the bus and ran full speed ahead down the sidewalk, racing past all of the other teenagers. *He's too fast. I'll never catch him.*

Finally, Gloria saw him: the one. A towhead moseyed off the bus, in no particular hurry. He shuffled down the sidewalk with a skateboard in hand. He set the skateboard on the sidewalk and hopped on.

Gloria hurried over. "Excuse me." The young man, whose hair was too long for Gloria's taste, turned dark green eyes on her. "Huh?"

Gloria pointed down the street. "You live here?"

"Uh-huh."

"Do you know most of the people who live on this street?" Maybe he was one of those nice young men that mowed lawns for extra cash in the summer...

He eyed her suspiciously. "What's it to you? You some kind of undercover cop?"

"No, I'm not, but I need your help." She fished inside her purse and pulled out a five-dollar bill. "I'm looking for someone – possibly a male – that lives in the neighborhood and walks with a limp."

The boy stared at the money.

"Here, take it," she urged.

The boy grabbed the five and shoved it in his back pocket. "Maybe." He eyed her open purse, waiting for more.

Gloria sucked in a deep breath and pulled out another five.

The teenage boy reached for it.

Gloria pulled it back, just as his fingers touched the edge. "Is there or isn't there?"

He eyed her thoughtfully as he rolled the skateboard back and forth with his foot. "Yeah, but I'm not sure of the name." He grabbed the second five and shoved it in his pocket.

"Is it a man or woman and can you point to the house?" she asked. Maybe she was finally getting somewhere!

"Who are you - Angela Lansbury?" he smirked.

Gloria gave him a dark look. "Don't get smart with me, young man! I have underwear older than you!"

The boy grinned. "Okay, just kidding. You don't have to get all turned up."

She raised a brow.

The boy rolled his eyes. "You know, worked up."

Gloria didn't know, nor did she care.

He jerked his head toward the row of houses. "Over there. The dude in that house has a limp. Most of the time, he walks with a cane."

Gloria followed his gaze. "The white house with black shutters?"

He nodded. "That's the one."

Finally! They had it narrowed it down.

Gloria grabbed a ten, the final bill she had tucked into the side of her purse and slapped it into his outstretched hand. "Thank you. You've been quite helpful."

The boy grinned, shoved the money in his pocket and adjusted his backpack. "You're welcome, granny."

She watched as he coasted down the sidewalk, eventually swerving into a driveway at the end of the street.

He picked up the board, tucked it under his arm and disappeared inside the house.

Gloria returned to the van and slid into the passenger seat. "We got a lead."

Ruth twisted in her seat. "Can I use the drone now?"

Gloria furrowed a brow. Although she believed the young man was telling the truth, it wouldn't hurt for her to see for herself that the man walked with a limp. She nodded. "Somehow, we need to get him outdoors."

Lucy leaned forward from the backseat. "That shouldn't be too difficult." She patted Ruth on the shoulder. "Ruth is dying to use her drone. Why don't we let her fly it down the street or something?"

Gloria studied Ruth's face. She could see the eager look in her friend's eyes. On top of that, Gloria had asked her bring it for a reason. "Fly away."

Ruth was never one to look a gift horse in the mouth and not wanting Gloria to change her mind and come up with a "Plan B," scrambled out of the van and scurried to the rear cargo door. She carefully pulled her drone from the back and carried it to the front of the van.

Gloria climbed out of the van. She, herself, was curious to see how the drone operated.

Ruth placed the drone on the cement sidewalk and pulled the controller from her purse.

Gloria glanced at her friend's face. She'd never seen her so excited, except maybe the time she had glued herself to her computer screen to spy on the post office! Yeah, the look was about the same.

"I think you missed your calling in life, Ruth," Gloria told her.

Ruth half-turned, her attention honed in on her precious piece of surveillance equipment. "Huh?"

"Never mind," Gloria mumbled.

Lucy climbed out of the van and stood next to Gloria.

Ruth took a step back, the controller gripped tightly in both hands.

"Whirr!" Small propellers, located on the four corners of the small machine, began to spin and the drone slowly lifted off the ground.

Ruth's face contorted as she concentrated on maneuvering the flying craft up into the air. Ruth steered it back and forth across the street as she practiced moving it along.

It lifted high in the air and then suddenly shot forward like a speeding bullet.

Ruth began to run as she tried to keep pace with her runaway machine.

Lucy cupped her hands to her mouth. "Pull back on the throttle," she yelled.

Ruth must have heard Lucy's advice as the drone suddenly slowed and began to hover over the center of the street.

Gloria and Lucy darted down the sidewalk to catch up with their friend.

The drone hovered about ten feet above them. "Time to move it into position," Ruth said.

Gloria frowned. "How much practice have you had with this?"

"I've only had it out once," Ruth admitted.

Gloria closed her eyes and offered a quick prayer that Ruth and her new toy wouldn't get them into trouble.

Lucy and Gloria followed close behind Ruth as she made her way across the street. She positioned herself off to the side, out of view of the suspect's house.

The women stepped off the sidewalk and slipped behind a cluster of tall juniper bushes at the edge of the property.

Off in the distance, Gloria could hear the faint "whirr" of the drone's propellers as it soared over the top of the six-foot privacy fence that separated the front of the yard from the rear.

Ruth shot out of the edge of the bush as she tried to keep a visual on her drone.

"Is it filming anything?" Lucy hissed.

Ruth shrugged. "I won't know for sure until I take a look at the memory card." She puckered her lips and narrowed her eyes. "I better bring it in. The battery is probably getting low."

Whoop. A faint "whooshing" sound came from behind the other side of the fence. "Uh-oh." Ruth's face fell.

"What?" Gloria whispered.

"I think the drone went down behind enemy lines." Ruth shoved the controls into Lucy's hands and darted across the yard.

Gloria cupped her hands to her lips. "What are you doing?" she hissed at Ruth.

"Going for the drone," she shot back, never slowing her pace.

Ruth grabbed the top of the dog-ear fence panel with both hands and hoisted herself onto the top of the panel. She teetered there for a long moment, half-in, half-out, her feet swinging wildly as she tried in vain to gain enough momentum to pull herself the rest of the way over.

"Help me!" she pleaded.

Gloria bolted across the lawn. She gave Ruth's feet one good shove and then they disappeared from sight.

"Umf."

Gloria peered through the crack in the wooden boards and caught sight of Ruth sprawled out, face down on the grass. "Hurry UP!" Gloria urged.

Ruth pulled herself up onto all fours and began to crawl across the yard. Her drone was a good eight feet away.

She had almost made contact with the drone when around the corner of the house, a pair of boots appeared.

"What is going on back here?" a male voice demanded.

Ruth's hand reached for the drone while her eyes traveled upwards. "I lost control of my drone," she explained breathlessly.

The man planted his feet apart, hands on hips. "You're trespassing," he growled.

"I am so sorry," Ruth apologized.

Lucy leaned over Gloria's shoulder as they watched in horror. "We need a distraction. Fast!"

She darted out into the street, her eyes searching frantically for a diversion. Her eyes fell upon a street drain. Lucy dropped to pavement and wedged her right foot between the top of the drain and metal grate.

Lucy sucked in a deep breath and screamed at the top of her lungs.

Gloria nearly jumped out of her skin! She spun around, her eyes falling on Lucy's small frame, sprawled out in the street.

She started to run over to help Lucy when Lucy frantically waved her away. "No!"

Gloria realized that Lucy had created a diversion, sprinted along the edge of the property line and disappeared behind the bushes.

The man looked down at Ruth and then towards the front of the house. He paused for a brief moment then disappeared inside, leaving Ruth and the drone behind.

He bolted out of his front door and made his way over to where Lucy, who was doing an excellent job of appearing to be in a dire situation, shrieked helplessly.

If the situation hadn't been so serious, Gloria would have burst out laughing. Lucy and helpless were two words Gloria would never use in the same sentence!

"I twisted my ankle and now my foot is wedged in the drain," she moaned.

She reached down and tugged on her calf. "Ahhhh! I think something is nibbling on my ankle!"

The man bent down and peered into the sewer. "I don't see anything. Hold still."

While his attention was on Lucy, Ruth grabbed her drone and ran to the rear of the yard. She caught a glimpse of Gloria as she ran along the other side. "Take the drone."

Before Gloria could answer, Ruth tossed the drone over the fence. Gloria lifted her hands above her head and grabbed onto the drone's propeller.

Ruth vaulted over the corner fence. Thankfully, the fence in the back was lower than the one that faced the front.

When Ruth was safely on the other side, Gloria hunched over and grabbed her friend's arm. "Let's get out of here."

They scurried across the rear neighbor's yard and onto the adjacent street. When they reached the safety of the street, Gloria let out a sigh of relief.

Meanwhile, Lucy, who still had the homeowner distracted, had one eye on the drain and one eye on Ruth's van parked at the front of the cul-de-sac.

"Just relax your leg," the man advised.

Lucy had tightened her calf muscle in attempt to make it seem as if her foot was truly stuck. She caught a glimpse of Ruth and Gloria as they opened the van doors and slipped inside.

She rubbed the side of her lower leg. "I think it's starting to come loose."

The man, using both hands, gently tipped her leg to the side and slowly pulled. Her foot "miraculously" freed itself from the inner drain and slid out.

Lucy blinked her eyes rapidly. "Oh thank you Mr. ..."

"Hendricks. Ron Hendricks."

"Mr. Hendricks," Lucy repeated. She lifted her pant leg and inspected her bare ankle. "Huh! I could've sworn something was gnawing on my flesh!"

She rolled over to her knees and slowly stood. She brushed her hands on the top of her pants and held out a hand. "Thank you so much."

"You're welcome." He pointed at the drain. "What in the world were you doing?"

Lucy waved dramatically. "I was searching for my dog, not paying attention to where I was going and my foot caught on something slippery. Next thing I know, I'm on the ground and my foot was wedged inside."

She went on. "When I felt something on my ankle, I panicked and when I tried to jerk my foot out, it wedged even tighter." She shuddered. "If you hadn't helped me, I would probably have rabies right now."

He glanced down the street. "You live around here?"

Lucy shook her head. "No...I live in B-." She corrected herself. "I live a few miles away and my dog seems to have wandered off so I'm checking all the neighborhoods."

"I haven't noticed any stray dogs," he said.

Before the man could ask more questions, Lucy turned to go. "I better keep looking."

She limped along the street, turning back once to watch Mr. Hendricks, whose limp was worse than Lucy's limp, make his way down the drive and back inside his house.

Lucy slid into the backseat, right next to Ruth, who had set up a small command post with her computer. She studied the screen. "I got some great footage of the suspect's backyard."

"Ron Hendricks," Lucy corrected.

Gloria grinned. "You got his name?"

Lucy nodded triumphantly. "Yep! Did you see his limp?"

Gloria gazed down the street. "Yes, I did. It's time to visit Paul with our evidence."

Chapter 24

After Ruth picked up the spy equipment from the house at 726 Pine Place, the women headed straight to the Montbay Sherriff station.

Luckily, Paul was at the station. He watched the drone footage in silence. "This is a good lead but it doesn't prove that he was the one that broke into the house and caused the damage."

He placed his reading glasses on the desk and leaned back in the chair. "What's his motive?"

Gloria frowned. True. The man lacked motive. He had opportunity and fit what little clues they had about the intruder.

Ruth closed her laptop and slid it back into her computer bag. "I wish I had been able to help crack the case," she said.

Gloria rose to her feet. "Do you mind if I borrow the card and take it home to study the footage?"

Ruth shrugged. "Sure. I have a spare at home."

She pulled the small memory card from a side pocket and placed it in Gloria's outstretched hand.

They rode back to Belhaven in silence. Gloria mulled over the clues they had. Why *would* someone intentionally sabotage a neighbor's home sale – unless they were enemies? From what the other neighbors had said, they had all been amicable, if not friends.

Back at the farm, she waited on the porch while Mally did her customary inspection of the yard and barns. Her eyes fell on the house across the street. It was a buzz of activity. Construction vans, electrical vans. It reminded her of Andrea's place.

When Mally finished, Gloria and she went inside. Her stomach grumbled. She opened the refrigerator door and peered inside. She had everything that was needed to make a sandwich but it seemed like she had been eating a lot of those lately.

She pulled out a small plastic grocery bag and untied the top. Inside was Alice's firehouse fajita. "Here goes nothing," she muttered under her breath.

She placed the fajita on a glass plate and then stuck the plate inside the microwave. Mally sat and watched the microwave intently. Gloria glanced down. "You will not like that," she told her.

Mally let out a low whine and flopped down onto the linoleum. "Alright," Gloria caved, "I'll give you a treat."

She pulled the packet of deli meat from the fridge and placed two slices on a paper plate. She tore a third piece into small bits and put those in Puddles' food dish. "I know you're not sick of ham," she said.

Mally and Puddles gulped their treats. After those were gone, they continued to watch Gloria's food cook. After the microwave turned off, she slid the plate from the oven and placed it on the table.

The scent of cilantro and Chile peppers drifted up, taunting Gloria. She eyed the piping hot fajita then headed back to the fridge where she grabbed a half gallon of milk. She poured a tall glass before she settled in at the table. "Maybe this will help offset the heat," she muttered under her breath.

The food was delicious and Gloria ate every single bite. She placed the dirty plate in the dishwasher and closed the door. The only plan she had for the rest of the evening was to go over what the drone had captured on camera earlier.

She made her way over to the computer and settled into the chair. Puddles waited for Gloria to settle in before he jumped onto her lap for a catnap.

Gloria fumbled around for several moments as she tried to remember where the small disk went. Finally, after she put her reading glasses on, she figured it out.

The file popped on the screen and Gloria clicked the tab. The first seconds of footage made Gloria dizzy as Ruth attempted to smooth out the drone's flight. There was no sound, just the recording.

When the video zoomed in then abruptly dropped close to the ground Gloria closed her eyes. She began to feel nauseous.

Gloria opened her eyes. The video had smoothed out. She was able to make out the suspect's backyard quite clearly. The drone zoomed haphazardly across the space before it plunked onto the grass when it ran out of battery power.

Mere seconds before it plunked to the ground and the screen went blank; Gloria caught a glimpse of something...something important.

She rewound the footage and played it again. She paused when she got to what she had noticed before. There it was. In plain sight...the link between Mr. Hendricks' house and the house across the street!

She darted to the kitchen for her cell phone. Gloria dialed her daughter's number, praying that she would answer and that she was with the home inspector.

"Hello?"

"Hi Jill. Are you still at the new house?" Gloria blurted out.

"Yeah." Jill covered the mouthpiece.

"Hello?"

Jill was back. "The inspector said he should be done in about 45 minutes," she explained. "You'll never guess who I ran into."

Gloria had no idea. "Who?"

"Sue Camp! She was showing another couple this house! Can you believe it?"

Somehow, Gloria could believe it. "Stay there! I think I have a break in the case." Before Jill could respond, Gloria disconnected the line and dialed Paul.

"I can link the intruder at 726 Pine Place to the neighbor across the street," Gloria told Paul. "Can you meet me at the house?"

"I'll call you right back."

Gloria paced the kitchen floor and waited. She needed Paul to be onboard, to show him the evidence. Otherwise, the suspect might get away and Jill would have a new neighbor who had no qualms about breaking into neighbors' homes.

The phone chirped. "So can you?" Gloria skipped the pleasantries.

"I'll be there in 30 minutes," he told her.

Gloria was halfway to the car when she remembered her laptop and the small disk. She placed both on the passenger seat, started the car and roared off down the road.

Paul was there when Gloria pulled in the drive. Jill's car was parked out front, along with another vehicle Gloria didn't recognize.

She grabbed her computer bag, slid out of the car and hurried up the steps. Paul met her at the front door. "I just got here."

He held the door while Gloria stepped inside. She could hear Jill's voice from somewhere in the back.

Gloria waved him to the dining room. "Take a look at this first."

She led him to the kitchen where she showed him the smashed cabinets and pointed to the gaping holes where the doors were missing.

Gloria placed her laptop bag on the kitchen counter, unzipped the cover and pulled it out.

305

She switched it on and clicked the icon for the video recording. "Watch the very end," she told him.

Paul leaned in and studied the video closely. At the end of the video footage, he noticed several cabinet doors, propped up against a wall inside a small storage area. The doors looked similar to the ones that were missing from 726 Pine Place. He hit the pause button. "I see them."

From where they were standing, they could look out the front picture window and had an unobstructed view of the house across the street. "I'll go have a chat with the neighbor." He looked at Gloria. "What's his name?"

"Ron Hendricks."

Paul nodded and then walked out the front door and across the street.

Gloria closed the lid on the computer and slid it into the bag as her daughter, Jill, and the inspector appeared from the hall.

She walked into the kitchen and hugged her mom. "I thought I heard your voice. What's up? Where did Paul go?"

Gloria nodded through the window. "He's having a chat with the neighbor."

The inspector interrupted. "I'll be in the basement checking mechanicals." He disappeared down the stairs.

"You're onto something," Jill said. "Please tell me you found something."

"We shall see," Gloria's eyes twinkled. The spark disappeared as she gazed at the gaping holes where cabinet doors were either missing or the intruder had smashed them.

Jill followed her mother into the kitchen. "Sue Camp said the owner's insurance is going to have all new kitchen cabinets installed before we move in and I get to pick them out!"

"So you get a new kitchen?"

Jill clasped her hands together and spun around. "I know, right?"

Gloria shifted the computer bag on her shoulder. "You mentioned Sue Camp was here showing the house to buyers?"

Jill crossed her arms. "Yes, and when I asked her what she was doing, she blew it off and said that if we backed out of the contract, she had several other backup offers."

"What a lovely woman," Gloria muttered.

Gloria caught a movement through the front window out of the corner of her eye. She stepped into the living room and watched as Paul lifted his radio to his lips. He stood in the drive across the street for several moments before he escorted Ron Hendricks down the drive and placed him in the back of his squad car.

Gloria and Jill waited at the door for Paul to return. "I'm taking Mr. Hendricks to the station for questioning. I need that disc," he told his fiancé.

Gloria pulled the small disk from the computer bag and dropped it into his hand.

"Thank you," he said.

She leaned forward and gave him a quick peck on the lips. "Thanks for being my knight in shining armor and coming to my rescue."

He grinned and winked. "Anything for my damsel in distress," he teased.

Jill rolled her eyes. "Oh brother!"

She turned to her mom. "That video...it has something to do with the guy across the street?"

"It's a long story, but Ruth was able to spy on the neighbor's backyard. The video she taped showed a stack of cabinet doors, identical to the ones missing from this kitchen, propped up in an open storage area behind his garage."

"On top of that, the footage of the break-in that Ruth's spy equipment recorded, tipped us off that the intruder had a limp, similar to Mr. Hendricks' limp."

Jill placed a hand on each side of her head. "But why? Why this house?"

Gloria tapped her foot on the floor. "That, my dear, is the million dollar question."

Chapter 25

Gloria was on pins and needles the rest of the day as she waited for Paul to let her know how Ron Hendricks' questioning had gone.

Gloria's number one priority was that Jill and her family move forward on the purchase of a new home.

Gloria was certain beyond a shadow of a doubt that the perpetrator had been uncovered and her daughter could safely move into the new home without worrying about someone breaking in.

She even offered to help Jill do a little painting before they moved although, in Gloria's book, painting was right up there with moving.

On her drive back to Belhaven, she noticed that Margaret had sent her a text message. When she got into town, she pulled off to the side of the road to read it.

"Stop by my place. Stat."

Gloria groaned inwardly. "Please, Lord. No more excitement, at least for a couple of days," she pleaded.

Instead of turning right at the stop sign on Main Street, she drove straight through town and up the hill toward Lake Terrace and Margaret's place.

Margaret's SUV was the only car in the drive and Gloria pulled Annabelle in behind it.

Margaret met her at the door. "It's here. It's *all* here!"

Gloria frowned as Margaret grabbed her hand and dragged her into the garage.

She flipped the light on. There, in the center of Margaret's garage, were several large boxes.

Gloria stepped forward. "What is all this?"

"Our surprises for the girls," Margaret exclaimed. "Remember? We decided to buy something special for each of them with our windfall?"

Gloria had been so wrapped up in Jill's house and the puppy mill; she had forgotten they were going to buy each of their close friends a special gift. Margaret hadn't forgotten.

"Bless your heart." Gloria impulsively reached over and hugged her friend. "You are the best!" she gushed.

Margaret blushed. "I tried. I know you have your hands full." She brightened. "So when do we get to surprise them?"

Now that Gloria had Jill's fiasco behind her, her mind began to clear. "The sooner the better." She snapped her fingers. "How about an afternoon tea at Magnolia Mansion? We can have Andrea and Alice put on our first shindig."

"Brilliant!" Margaret agreed. "I'm so excited." She rubbed her hands together.

"Remind me what we picked out again," Gloria said.

Margaret ticked off each of the surprises and it all came back to Gloria.

They had picked out the perfect gifts. There was only one problem. "What about Andrea?"

Margaret's mouth formed an "O" as she realized that they hadn't purchased anything for their young friend.

Andrea didn't "need" anything. When Andrea's husband, Daniel, had died, she collected a large amount of money from a hefty life insurance policy. On top of that, she had recently sold the insurance agency so that she could focus on the Magnolia Mansion Tearoom.

Their young friend had also started dabbling in interior design, which Gloria decided was the perfect fit for Andrea.

If Andrea wanted something, she could just go out and buy it.

Gloria stared at the tower of gifts in Margaret's garage. There were special gifts for each of the Garden Girls. It suddenly dawned on Gloria – the perfect gift for Andrea. "I've got it!"

She explained her idea to Margaret, who nodded eagerly. "That's perfect. Hers will be the best gift of all," Margaret predicted.

Gloria promptly called Andrea. "Yes, dear. I'm here with Margaret and we would like to plan a special afternoon at the tea room...a private party for the Garden Girls."

After she hung up the phone, she grinned at Margaret. "All set for this Sunday afternoon. All we need now is to get everyone rounded up at the same time."

Margaret interrupted. "You work on Andrea's gift and I'll take care of the other."

Paul called just as Gloria was getting back into her car. "What happened?" She couldn't wait to find out.

"Ron Hendricks confessed," Paul told her. "With a little strong arm," he added.

"But why? Why target that house?" That was the big question.

Paul went on to explain that Ron Hendricks and Marco Acosta had had a falling out. It all started when Mr. Hendricks purchased a puppy – a purebred Labrador retriever – from Acosta. When the dog became ill and Hendricks had to spend hundreds of dollars, only to have the dog die, hard feelings surfaced.

One day, not long after the dog died, Hendricks chased one of his other dogs across the street and into Acosta's yard where he fell into a deep hole. His ankle broke in several spots and after numerous painful surgeries, the doctors told him he would never walk again without a noticeable limp.

Paul switched the phone to his other ear. "He believed that Acosta had intentionally booby-trapped his backyard so that Hendricks would

316

get hurt. The Acosta family moved shortly after the accident and that was when Hendricks hatched a plan for revenge."

"Wow, talk about bad blood," Gloria said.

"Yes. It's up to Marco Acosta if he wants to pursue legal action," Paul told her.

After Gloria hung up the phone, she backed Annabelle out of Margaret's drive and headed through town, in the opposite direction of the farm and home.

She had two stops to make for Andrea's special gift. The first one was Trinkets and Treasures, the oddities shop in nearby Green Springs. She was certain they would have just what she was looking for!

Chapter 26

The rest of the week flew by and before Gloria knew it, Sunday morning had arrived. She woke up early, anxious to hear Pastor Nate's message, a continuation of a series he had recently started on the Book of Revelation and the tribulation. Today was also the day that Margaret and she planned to surprise the girls with their gifts.

Gloria stepped inside the sanctuary and started down the center aisle. She stopped to hug her friend, Ruth, who had been instrumental in solving the intruder mystery.

Then she stopped to hug Dot, who said she had some good news from the doctors and would share it later when they all met at Andrea's for the party.

Andrea and Alice scooched across the bench seat to make room for Gloria. She had just settled into her seat when the choir began to sing and she stood back up.

Some Sunday mornings the music was upbeat and cheerful. Other Sundays, it was more solemn worship music. Today was the slower, more reverent hymns of praise.

Gloria blinked back sudden tears as the music touched her heart. Andrea must have felt the same. She reached over and squeezed her friend's hand.

Pastor Nate's message was both stirring and thought provoking. Gloria made a mental note to study the key scripture from Revelation:

"Truly I tell you, this generation will certainly not pass away until all these things have happened. Heaven and earth will pass away, but my words will never pass away.

But about that day or hour no one knows, not even the angels in heaven, nor the Son, but only the Father. Be on guard! Be alert! You do not know when that time will come. Mark 13: 30 – 33. NIV

After the service ended, the girls wandered outdoors to their usual meeting spot. Gloria shivered as a brisk November wind tugged at the collar of her shirt and gave her a taste of what was to come.

Andrea felt it too, as she stomped her shiny, black designer shoe on the cement. "Brr!"

The meeting was brief since the girls would be gathering at Andrea's place in a few short hours. Gloria caught Margaret's eye and winked.

Lucy and Ruth offered to visit the shut-ins since Andrea had to prep for the party, Dot had to cover at the restaurant for a few hours before the girls met, and Gloria and Margaret had to gather all their goodies and take them to Andrea's place.

Andrea had a hunch the girls were up to something but she wasn't about to spoil the fun so she kept mum about what little she did know.

Gloria and Margaret met at Andrea's place right after lunch.

When they stepped inside the sunroom, Gloria gasped. Tiny twinkling lights illuminated the large, towering trees Andrea had strategically placed about the room.

Several small bistro tables, covered with an array of pastel-colored cloths, sat clustered together in one section. Andrea had put them together so that all of the girls could sit next to one another.

Margaret and Gloria carried the boxes of goodies into the room and set them off in the corner. Andrea raised a brow when she saw the huge stack.

Alice slid in front of Andrea and clucked. "What is this? Christmas?"

Margaret rubbed her hands together. Not wanting to leave Alice out, Margaret had managed to find a special gift for her, too.

After the girls finished unloading the boxes, they wandered into the kitchen. Lined up on the counter were several rows of mouth-watering, tempting morsels.

"Try one," Andrea urged.

Gloria plucked one from the plate and nibbled the edge. Tangy Dijon mustard tickled her tongue. She pulled it back to inspect the contents. It was a slice of French bread and on top of the bread was a piece of salty ham and brie cheese.

Margaret selected watercress. It was the perfect finger food. "This is delicious," she exclaimed.

Andrea smiled. "Are you sure?"

"Absolutely," Gloria reassured her friend.

Alice pulled a smaller side tray to the front. "Now you must try this," she declared.

The tray was loaded with bite-size tortilla chips. Gloria lifted a small chip, shaped like a cup and studied the mixture inside.

Alice rattled off the ingredients. "Black beans, salsa, cream cheese and green onion."

Gloria gobbled the tasty morsel and grabbed a paper napkin to wipe her lips. "This is so good! By the way, I ate my firehouse fajita yesterday for lunch and it was delicious."

Alice beamed with pride. "You like? I make you more."

Andrea held up a hand to stop her. "But not today. We have our hands full," she reminded her.

"Si," Alice agreed.

Finally, the hour arrived and the rest of the Garden Girls straggled in, hanging their coats on a beautiful antique coat rack that Gloria hadn't noticed before. It was beautiful and looked old.

"Where did you get this?" Gloria asked.

Andrea ran her hand down the smooth, solid oak coat rack. "I've been rummaging around estate sales. You should go with me sometime. They have lots of cool stuff."

Gloria grinned and shook her head. "I'm sure it's a lot of fun but I'm trying to get *rid* of my things, not accumulate more," she pointed out.

"True," Andrea agreed.

The girls oohed and aahed over the tasty treats that Alice and Andrea had worked so hard to create. They gushed at the beautiful decorations and Andrea beamed like the proud manor owner that she now was!

Finally, the goodies consumed, everyone turned their attention to Dot. Gloria spoke first. "First and foremost, how are you Dot?"

All eyes turned to their friend.

Dot's eyes traveled around the room as she focused on each of her dear friends. Tears threatened to spill as she thought about how they had pitched in to help and how much they all meant to her. "I-I'm going to be fine. They caught the cancer early and with a little treatment after the surgery, I should be cancer-free before you know it."

A collective sigh of relief filled the room. The women impulsively joined hands as Gloria prayed. "Thank you, Dear God, for Dot's good news. We pray for continued healing in her life as she moves through treatment and thank You for answering our prayers."

A unanimous AMEN erupted and Alice ran out to grab a fresh pot of hot water. She moved quickly since she couldn't wait to find out what kind of goodies the girls had brought to surprise their friends.

Margaret and Gloria made their way around the cluster of tables and stood near the divider that hid the gifts from sight.

The room grew quiet as the rest of the girls wondered what they were doing. Gloria nodded to Margaret.

"As you know, Gloria and I were fortunate enough to stumble on those rare coins in the mountains when we were chasing after Liz." She glanced around the room. "Gloria and I decided that there was no one else in the world we would rather share our unexpected gift with – than you – our dearest friends."

She paused and Gloria picked up. "So, without further ado, we have something special for each of you."

Margaret and Gloria slid the partition to the side to reveal the tall stack of boxes.

The girls gasped in surprise.

"Ruth first," Margaret said.

Ruth paused for just a moment before she jumped out of her chair and crossed the room.

Gloria grabbed one box and Margaret reached for a second.

Gloria held out her box. "Inside this box is the ultimate spy package. It includes a spy pen with audio recording, a set of GPS tracking devices in case you need more than one and an amplifier to hook up to the surveillance you already have so you don't have to use ear buds."

Ruth's eye lit up and Gloria could tell she was ready to rip the box open. "We're not done."

Margaret held out the larger box. "This is the deluxe Phantom II drone with longer range, a battery that can last up to an hour and more camera time."

Ruth clutched her chest. "Really? Oh my gosh! How did you know I wanted the Phantom II?"

"Kenny," Gloria explained. "He told us you wanted it but it was out of your price range."

Ruth impulsively kissed Gloria's cheek first and then Margaret's.

"Thank you, Ruth, for letting me use your drone to crack Jill's case," Gloria added gratefully.

Ruth floated back to her seat, the larger of the two boxes securely in her grasp.

Gloria placed her other box off to the side. "Don't forget this later."

Ruth shook her head. "Are you kidding me?"

Margaret snapped her fingers. "Oh, and one more thing. Inside that box is the name and number of a company in Grand Rapids that retrofits vehicles with special equipment. We've already paid to have your van equipped with state-of-the-art spy equipment for mobile use."

Ruth placed her hands on both sides of her cheeks. "I think I just died and went to heaven."

The group of friends giggled at Ruth's reaction. Truly, Margaret and Gloria had given her the perfect gift.

"Dot, you're next," Gloria waved her to the front.

Dot shuffled to the front of the room.

Gloria reached for her hand. "The best gift ever is the good news from the doctors." A tear slid down Dot's cheek, then Margaret's cheek. Soon, all of the women were crying and Andrea darted out of the room in search of Kleenex as she wiped at her wet eyes.

Gloria cleared her throat and smiled through her tears. "We know that the old stove in your restaurant has been on the fritz for a while now so," she turned to Margaret, "so we bought you the best commercial grade oven and stove we could find." She thrust a stack of papers in Dot's hand. "All you have to do is call the number on the sheet and they will schedule the delivery."

"I-I." Dot closed her mouth, afraid she would become unglued and then they would all be bawling again.

"You're welcome." The women all got out of their chairs and surrounded their friend.

Finally, when the hugs and the tears subsided, Dot sat back down and Gloria pointed to Lucy. "You're next."

Lucy grinned and jumped to her feet.

When Lucy got close, Margaret began to speak. "We tried to get you a lifetime supply of sweets but no one could handle the order."

The girls giggled and Lucy frowned.

"We hope you like what we came up with instead," Gloria told her. She handed her a box. "We bought you a lifetime supply of ammo for your guns."

Margaret held out an envelope, "And we arranged for a company to come out and build you your own custom shooting range."

Lucy grinned from ear-to-ear. "Are you kidding me?" She spun around and faced Andrea, who also liked to target practice at Lucy's place in her free time. "Did you hear that? We're getting a new shooting range?" She grabbed the envelope and lifted it to her lips. "Whoopee!" She bounced back to her seat.

Gloria had a fleeting thought that she might one day regret the decision to build her friend a shooting range. She would have to worry about that another day.

The girls gazed at the small pile of gifts behind Margaret and Gloria.

A twinge of jealousy shot through Andrea, although she quietly dismissed it. This was a special day for the Garden Girls. Maybe someday...

Gloria reached down and grabbed the larger of the two boxes left on the floor. "We have something for you, Alice."

Alice pointed to her chest. "Me?"

Margaret nodded. She motioned her to come.

Alice looked at Andrea uncertainly and Andrea nodded. "Go!" she urged.

Alice wandered to the front.

Gloria held out the box. "There are two things in this box." She turned to Margaret who held up a finger.

"First, there is a year's supply of ghost chili." Alice clapped her hands. "Oh, the dishes I can make!"

"Second, is a simulated driving course so you can learn to drive while watching TV," Gloria added.

Alice beamed. "Oh, I will use it every day, Miss Gloria," Alice promised. She gave each of them a hug before she made her way to the back of the room.

Andrea picked up an empty dish and started for the door.

She took a step back when Gloria stopped her. "Wait, Andrea. We haven't given you your gift yet."

Andrea paused. "Me?"

Gloria smiled. "Why, of course."

All five of the friends turned to Andrea, still standing in the back. Gloria waved her up. "Come get your gift," she urged.

Andrea slowly made her way to the front as Margaret picked up the last box. It was the smallest of them all but it held the most significance to each of the five Garden Girls, for each of them knew what the box held. It was a special gift and they waited eagerly for Gloria to explain.

Gloria didn't explain. Instead, she simply handed the box to Andrea. "Open it."

The box was unlike the rest, meticulously and lovingly wrapped in a bright, shiny paper. Tied in the center was a bright green bow. Pictures of gardening gloves, packets of seeds and small green plants covered the outside.

The paper was beautiful. Andrea pried the tape off with her fingernail and carefully set the paper and bow to the side. She lifted the lid on the box and pulled out the only thing that was inside...a green hat. A Garden Girls hat, not unlike the one that Margaret, Lucy, Dot, Ruth and Gloria had purchased when they formed their Garden Girls Club.

"Welcome to the club," Gloria simply said.

Andrea stared at the hat, then up at her friend. "You mean..."

"Welcome to the club," the five women, who had unanimously voted to add Andrea to their small group, exclaimed.

Andrea popped the hat on her head and beamed with pride. The hat was the best gift ever!

The other three made their way to the front as each of them hugged their young friend. She had been a part of the group for a while now, at least in their hearts and minds, and now it was official!

Alice stood near the back and took a picture of the five – now six – women, with Andrea near the middle, grinning from ear-to-ear.

After Alice finished taking several pictures and the women cleared the clutter, Gloria stopped them one more time.

"We have one more gift," Margaret announced. "This one is for *all* of us."

Gloria nodded. "We commissioned an artist from Grand Rapids to paint The Garden Girls portrait and if Andrea doesn't mind, we would love to hang it here at Magnolia Mansion."

The girls were thrilled and Andrea, too, since she would be able to display it in the tearoom for all to enjoy. "After our painting, we commissioned him to paint one more – of Magnolia Mansion - and you can put that anywhere you like," Gloria said.

The chatter of excited voices filled the sunroom and spilled over into the rest of the house. This house promises years of wonderful memories for not only Andrea, but also the rest of the Garden Girls.

Margaret and Gloria were the last to leave. Gloria flung her arm around Margaret's shoulder. "Well done, my friend," she said.

Margaret paused. "You, too." She slid the tip of her high heel pump across the smooth tile floor. "You know, the best gift we have is each other."

"That is the truth." Gloria hugged Margaret and then watched as she made her way down the drive to her SUV before heading to the kitchen.

She wanted to thank Andrea one last time for making the day special.

Andrea, still wearing her green hat, was in the kitchen covering the leftovers.

Gloria tapped the tip of the hat. "I take it you are happy with our gift."

"I think she will sleep with it on her head," Alice predicted.

Gloria smiled.

Alice wiped her hands on her apron. "Oh! Miss, Gloria. In all the excitement, I forgot about the Acosta family. You know, the people with all the dogs."

Gloria frowned. She had forgotten as well. "You said you had a chance to talk to them."

"Si. Perhaps if you are free in a day or two, we can go out there to talk to the owners."

Gloria nodded. The sooner the better. She had vowed to help those poor animals and that was what she was going to do.

"How about tomorrow? If you can reach the owners, we can swing by there tomorrow."

"Yes. That is good," Alice agreed.

Finally, Gloria the last to leave headed to the car. The sun had set and with all the excitement of the last couple of days, she was ready to spend a quiet evening at home, kicking back in her recliner and watching her favorite detective show.

She pulled Annabelle into the drive and climbed out of the car. Brilliant streaks of cotton candy pink and tangerine orange filled the skies across the street... God's magnificent creation.

Gloria locked the car doors and headed inside. She smiled and looked back one last time at the sky. God had surely blessed Gloria and she couldn't wait for what tomorrow would bring.

***

The end...or is it? I tossed around the idea of leaving a taste of what was to come in Book #9...and decided to leave it up to you – my reader. If you are content with the tidy ending, read no further.

If you would like to take a peek at Gloria's upcoming adventure, feel free to turn the page for the second ending.

Happy Reading and Have a Blessed Day!

Hope

Visit my website for new releases and special offers: HopeCallaghan.com

If you enjoyed reading "Bully in the 'Burbs, please take a moment to leave a review. It would be greatly appreciated! Thank you!

The series continues...look for Book #9 in November, 2015

Gloria pulled Annabelle into the drive and climbed out of the car. Brilliant streaks of cotton candy pink and tangerine orange filled the skies...God's magnificent creation.

Gloria, distracted by the beauty that surrounded her, almost missed the police car and crime scene van parked in front of the farmhouse across the road. Almost.

The end, end!

Monster Cookies

Ingredients

½ cup brown sugar
¼ cup white sugar
½ cup margarine, softened
1 cup peanut butter
3 eggs
2 tsp. vanilla
4 ½ cup rolled oats
2 tsp. baking soda
4 oz. chocolate chips
4 oz. M&M candies
½ cup chopped walnuts or pecans

Directions

Preheat oven to 350 degrees.
Cream together sugars, softened margarine and peanut butter.
Add eggs and vanilla.
Beat well
Mix together oats and baking soda.
Add to creamed mixture.
Stir in chocolate chips, candy and walnuts.
Mix all ingredients thoroughly.
Drop by teaspoonful onto greased cookie sheet.
Bake at 350 degrees for 10 minutes.

About The Author

Hope Callaghan is an author who loves to write Christian books, especially Christian Mystery and Cozy Mystery books. Born and raised in a small town in West Michigan, she now lives in Florida with her husband.

She is the proud mother of one daughter and a stepdaughter and stepson. When she's not doing the thing she loves best - writing books - she enjoys cooking, traveling and reading books.

Hope loves to connect with her readers!

Visit hopecallaghan.com for information on special offers and soon-to-be-released books!

Email: hope@hopecallaghan.com

Facebook page:
http://www.facebook.com/hopecallaghanauthor

Other Books by Author, Hope Callaghan:

DECEPTION CHRISTIAN MYSTERY SERIES:

Waves of Deception: Samantha Rite Series Book 1
Winds of Deception: Samantha Rite Series Book 2
Tides of Deception: Samantha Rite Series Book 3

GARDEN GIRLS CHRISTIAN COZY MYSTERIES SERIES:

Who Murdered Mr. Malone? Garden Girls Mystery Series Book 1
Grandkids Gone Wild: Garden Girls Mystery Series Book 2
Smoky Mountain Mystery: Garden Girls Mystery Series Book 3
Death by Dumplings: Garden Girls Mystery Series Book 4
Eye Spy: Garden Girls Mystery Series Book 5
Magnolia Mansion Mysteries: Garden Girls Mystery Series Book 6
Missing Milt: Garden Girls Mystery Series Book 7
Bully in the 'Burbs: Garden Girls Mystery Series Book 8
Book 9 Coming November 2015! **HopeCallaghan.com**
Garden Girls Christian Cozy Mysteries Boxed Set Books 1-4

CRUISE SHIP CHRISTIAN COZY MYSTERIES SERIES:

Starboard Secrets Cruise Ship Cozy Mysteries Book 1
Portside Peril: Cruise Ship Cozy Mysteries Book 2
Lethal Lobster: Cruise Ship Cozy Mysteries Book 3
Book 4 Coming October 2015! **HopeCallaghan.com**

64989328R00208

Made in the USA
Lexington, KY
29 June 2017